MW01017350

GALAXY'S
END

J.T. SOLO

Galaxy's End

Future House Publishing

ISBN: 978-1-944452-97-1

Developmental editing by Erin Searle
Substantive editing by Sara Ansted
Copy editing by Abbie Robinson
Interior design by McKinli Wall

PART ONE
PICA

CHAPTER 1

The Tactum was the subspace communication link between a thousand worlds. And ever since it had joined one solar system to another over five hundred years ago, the Tactum had carried the voices of the citizens of the Cooperative across the vast expanse between stars instantaneously. It enabled the colonization of the galaxy.

And it had never gone silent. Until right now.

So when the lights began to fall from the sky, Dax was... mildly perturbed.

"Tai," he said, turning to his second, who was on the tactical console, "I think our T-receiver is acting up." He tapped on a silhouette on the ship display. "I am not receiving an albedo body from the Luxuria."

"Acting up?" Tai said, not looking up from her console. "That would suggest that our T-receiver was ever acting—."

"Acting down?" Dax suggested.

"Acting nominally," Zeph said from his navigation console. "The word you want is 'nominal.'"

"Thank you, astrogator," Tai said. "Nominal. Which would mean that you would actually need enough money to fix it or buy a new one. Who ever heard of a transport ship without a spare receiver?" She paused. "Or any ship, for that matter."

"We could afford a new receiver and as many spares as you'd like, if we didn't have to shell out on extravagances like crew pay, or food, or—"

"Or O2 scrubbers," Tai said. Still not looking up from her tac console.

"Yes, extravagances like breathing oxygen. If we could otherwise skip all of those, yes, we could afford a new receiver."

"And spares," Zeph said.

"Well, it's not the receiver," Tai said. "This time," she added. "I just ran a diagnostic and the reason you aren't seeing an albedo body is because she isn't reflecting one. At least not one we are picking up." Albedo bodies were a very useful form of navigation, even if they were light minutes or hours old. Within the system they acted as extra points of reference to the local stars and planets.

"Well it's not like she just magically cloaked herself," he said. "I mean, she can't right?"

"The Luxuria is an Aphrodite class star line cruise ship." Tai said, looking at the screen more closely. "She most definitely does not have stealth capabilities."

"Okay, so she went somewhere." Dax tapped his chin. "Zeph, give me positions, last broadcasted." They were going to crash into something, knowing their luck.

"On it." Zeph keyed in a sequence on his console, the blue bridge overhead lights contrasting with the orange glow of the console. "What the—wow."

"I don't like that wow." Dax walked over to Zeph's seat. "That's not a good wow."

"Well, I just tried pulling the last known local storage from Kyrie's memory into the navcom." The navigation computer had one of the most powerful processors on the ship. "And I couldn't."

"Wait, we lost the data?"

"No the data is there, it just can't be pulled into the navcom." Zeph squinted at his screen for a moment. "I'm going to hardwire it." He got out of his seat. "Tai, you sure the T-receiver isn't down? This is just like when it went down two runs ago, when the—"

"I'm pretty voiding sure it's working. The reason that we aren't seeing her albedo body is because it just ain't voiding there." She threw her readout on the main display. "Look for yourself."

There was a pause as Dax tried make sense of what he was

seeing. And not seeing.

"Uh, Tai, unless every ship, station, and planet in the system just learned how to turn their albedo down to 0, something is odd here." He turned to Zeph. "You slaved the ship memory to navcom yet?"

"Wires! What, we back in the petroleum age now? We gonna start burning fossil fuels to drive combustion engines to . . ." his voice trailed off to a muffle as he got farther into the navcom's chassis.

Moments later, his head popped up. "There we go, I plugged it into the rest of the ship. With wires. Like a peasant." He patted the navcom fondly, though, before closing up. "But, I guess we're lucky this ship is basically an ancient relic. Hardwired main systems? In another ship, you'd be dead in the void if the receiver went down."

Tai said, "I told you the receiver isn't down!" the same time Dax said, "You knockin' my ship, Zeph?"

The Kyrie had been a light military transport before it was converted to just a light transport. A very old light military transport.

"Well?" Dax gestured to the main screen. "What do you got for me?"

"I don't know boss. Last broadcasted is at least a few minutes old now."

"Cap, something strange here." The tone in Tai's voice sent a small shiver down Dax's spine. "I'm not receiving any visual telemetry."

"So she went invisible and silent?" Dax asked.

"No, I mean I am not receiving any visual telemetry from anything. In the system." Tai locked eyes with Dax.

"Hammers," Dax responded. Tai usually reserved that look for extremely bad situations. Which was pretty much any time Dax was involved in whatever local system's variant of poker was available. "Tai, extend our receivers. I want raw visual feed on the display." He turned to Zeph. "Give me interpolation, last known. Don't worry about when the live data cuts off, just calculate from the last two hours of the feed."

Kyrie's main display went dark just as the bridge went silent. The only sound was the navcom's ALU crunching the data.

The screen lit up.

"What in the voids," Tai said.

Dax framed an albedo body with his fingers and pulled his hands apart to expand on the image. There was a nav marker labeled Luxuria but the red hash marks encircled empty space where there should have been star liner.

From where they stood, just a little over thirty light seconds away from Pica 3, she was simply a white albedo body against space's dark background.

"She's falling into the gravity well," Tai said. They waited a few more moments, watching the body of reflected light move slowly closer to the planet. "With her mass, very soon she'll be so deep down Pica 3's well that she won't be able to escape without planetary tugs"

"Something must be wrong," Dax said. "Zeph overlay comms. What are they reporting? Engine failure? Hull breach?"

"I have no signal. It's all static."

"Bounce off the nearest sat relay, get the comm data from there." Dax pointed to the relay's nav marker on screen."

"No boss, you don't understand. It's all static. I'm not getting a single ping or bounce from anything."

Dax turned to look at Zeph, the disbelief turning into acid in his stomach. "That's impossible."

Zeph nodded. "Nothing." There was a slight hint of panic in Zeph's voice.

"Look—no escape pods, no stabilizers or retro thrusters firing…nothing." Tai was using their accrued visual feed from the last few minutes to compile an upscaled image. "It can't be structural, there isn't any atmo venting. They're just free falling."

"Not just the Luxuria," Zeph said.

There were several other bodies on the display that were accelerating to nearby gravity wells. It hadn't been apparent before, because they were light minutes and hours further away, but it was clear now.

"What's happening to them?" Tai asked. "And why isn't it

happening to us?"

"Tai, you said for sure that our T-receiver wasn't down."

"For the last time, Cap," Tai started.

"And Zeph, still nothing over comms?"

"I wouldn't lie to you, boss."

Dax looked at the display. No updated visual telemetry. No updated navigational telemetry. He turned to look at their navcom. And the fiber optic cable that Zeph had ran from computer to the ship.

"No voiding way."

CHAPTER 2

"Zeph, what did you say again, about being lucky?" Dax pointed at Zeph while snapping his fingers.

"Usually I'm talking about us being unlucky," Zeph said. "Like, extremely unlucky. Which is ironic if you consider that one third of the crew has a gambling addiction."

"No, you said that 'it was lucky that the ship . . .'" It was on the tip of Dax's tongue. ". . . Something?"

Zeph thought for a moment. "Lucky the ship is an ancient relic?"

"Hey—"

"Classic?"

"Lucky how?"

"Because the main systems are hardwired. Which is great because you never get a spare receiver for the Kyrie, and one day we're going to—"

"Why is that lucky?" Dax said, cutting Zeph off. "More importantly why does it make those other ships unlucky?"

"A ship the size of the Luxuria can't wire all its systems together. Voids, a ship the fraction of the size couldn't: that would be hundreds of miles of wire. And you can't use radio or other electromagnetic frequencies if you want to operate near jump speeds. So they piggyback off the Tactum to allow the different systems to interface with each other."

"How about redundancies, fail-safes?" Dax asked.

"You just reroute," Zeph said, "through an adjacent T-network. Or, if needed, cross over to a T-network in parallel."

"Okay," Dax said, still playing this mind game, still watching albedo bodies on the display slowly drift into gravity wells. "What if their T-receivers go down?"

"No, I don't think you understand," Zeph said. "Ships of a large enough size, the whole ship is one Tactum receiver and transmitter. That's why it's so convenient. No wires at all. Instant transfer, total coverage."

"What if the Tactum was to magically…I don't know…" Dax couldn't believe he was going to say this. "What if the Tactum went down?"

"The Tactum…?

"Went down," Dax finished. "Stopped existing."

"That would be like assuming that magnetism magically stopped existing. Or gravity. Or some other force of nature."

Zeph looked really perturbed. "I mean, it's like Tai said. They piggyback off the Tactum, the entire ship network. Every other system in the ship would be unable to communicate to any other. Wedge drive to telemetry. Life support to habitat control."

"Navigation to engines," Tai said, gesturing to the slowly falling albedo bodies.

"So what about doing what you did?" Dax asked, gesturing to Zeph. "Ad hoc hardwire?"

"You got a mile a fiber optic just lying around? Who knows, maybe the Luxuria does. Either way it would take them hours to lay it down."

"So if the Tactum is really down . . ." Dax paused. He couldn't go down that line of thinking right now. "So what can we do?" Dax asked.

"About what?" Zeph looked at him quizzically.

"About that!" He gestured to the scene unfolding on the display screen in front of them. "We have to do something!"

"Do what?" Zeph said. He pulled the specs of the Luxuria, and then for good measure, threw the specs of the Kyrie next to it. "We're a percentage of a fraction of the ship's mass tonnage. And how many people could we even hold? Not to mention life support, which I should remind you we are trying to replenish."

"It doesn't matter!" How could he explain it to Zeph, who had never spacefared out of the set routes they traveled?

"When it all goes to hell out here, there's isn't Cooperative or Republic, inner systems or rim. There's only the Void and us."

He turned to Tai. She nodded. "I'm prepping tight beam. Maybe we can communicate that we are trying to render assistance." She keyed commands to her console. "Zeph, let's receive on wide range, see if anyone is broadcasting in the clear."

Zeph shook his head. "Wide Range. Tight Beam." More head shaking. "Jeezawow. It's a testament to this ship's . . ." he gave a pause as Dax tried to shoot him the coldest warning glare he could muster, "'classic-ness' that it still even has those, uh, classic devices."

"Just, do what you can. I'm going hands on."

Zeph shook his head again, muttering something about "hands-on", "combustion engines" under his breath.

Tai leaned in from her console. "Dax, obviously we have to do what we can, but what if, and this strains all credulity to say, but if the Tactum is really down and this isn't just a solar system wide fluke, we are going to have bigger problems to deal with."

"Then we'll deal with it when we know for sure that there isn't anyone we can help on that whole cruiser." Dax gripped the ship controls. "I'm going hands on."

The ship came to life. She had been drifting aimlessly when the positional sats stopped broadcasting navigational telemetry. It felt particularly odd to Zeph to be hands on inside the solar system's main axis.

"Zeph, give me interpolation on screen." Zeph keyed his console, and the main view window was now superimposed with interpolation data using last known details of ships, planets, moons, and other notable bodies in the solar system, even if they were outside visual range. "Hopefully we'll be able to get some visuals on anything before it's too late to get out of its way."

"Blind leading the blind here," Zeph said.

Dax prepared himself for some very stressful light minutes.

CHAPTER 3

Except for the planets and moons, most of the ID tags circled empty space, the ships have either left, or captured by a nearby gravity well. As they got closer to the Luxuria, they started seeing the albedo bodies of some smaller ships that were light minutes away.

"Any hails on the open frequencies?" Tai asked.

"None, but that doesn't surprise me. Most smaller ships don't have any long-range transmitters that aren't the T-kind." He read some data off his console. "But in a few moments, we should be within tight beam range."

"Zeph, can you give me their telemetry on screen? I want to get us to relative stop with her, if not synchronous orbit." Matching velocity would be hard enough without trying to match rotation as well.

Zeph complied, and Dax finessed the Kyrie into drifting

at a rather steady 2000 kilometers from the star cruiser.

Tai pointed to a slowly forming albedo body on the screen. "Is that another ship?"

Zeph squinted at the screen. "I'm going to attempt a tight beam." In absence of the Tactum, they would have to depend on the line of sight data feed. Zeph fingers flew across the console. Dax couldn't imagine the on the fly adjustments Zeph was making, trying to guess the position of a ship from only the after image of reflections light seconds away. After a few tense seconds, Zeph grinned. "I got a ping. I'm going to send a handshake request!"

The two smaller ships danced a graceful tango around the cruiser, trying to maintain relative stopping while also establishing a line of sight for their tight beam transmission. "Handshake established!" Zeph said, triumph clear in his voice. "They're sending over their—"

The ship exploded.

"Six bullets and a funeral. Where did that come from?" Dax had the controls in a death grip, trying to look for a source of the attack.

An alarm went off on Tai's console. "It's radiological."

"Someone shot a fissile grade projectile? Out here?" They were practically blind, the visual feed only illuminating and displaying a small fraction of the space surrounding them. The visual feed started to distort. "Great, radiation interference."

Tai squinted at something in her screen. "Something's wrong."

"You mean in addition to a ship being blown up by a missile?"

"That's what's wrong. The radiological signature isn't that of a typical payload. In its mostly unspent fissile material. Not the kind you explode, but the kind you—oh no."

Dax peeled his eyes away from the display screen, looking for their phantom killer, to stare at Tai. "What?"

"Amaterasu."

In horror, Dax rotated the display to show the sun.

The Pica solar system was a green system, deriving most of their energy from renewable sources, specifically the Amaterasu solar fusion farm. It was a massive lase-like structure that surrounded the smaller of the two suns, Pica Solara minor.

"It's chain reacting."

"That's impossible, Amaterasu control station is supposed to monitor th—"

Tai shook her head. No Tactum. No T-drones. No way to control the energy output.

"Zeph, start spinning up the Wedge drive and let's make like a tree and get out of here!" He looked at the Luxuria, silent as a tomb. No life pods leaving her. He pounded his fist into his thigh, trying to shock some of the numbness out of him.

"Spinning up to where?"

"I don't know? I do know there are going to be a few thousand asteroid sized nuclear missiles that are going to be exploding from Pica Solara minor and they are going to rip through this tiny transport ship. It's a wonder that we didn't already get hit by some space trash or collided with a random satellite. They were literally midstream of the main transport route."

"I don't have any live navigational feed to calculate off of." Zeph starting spinning up calculations anyway. "And if I use the local storage, it'll be off by light minutes, if not more. We could wedge right into another ship."

More alarms went off on Tai's console. "Critical radiological warning, Cap."

"The probability of dying in the other side of the solar system—" He gestured to the image of the rapidly degrading sun—"is a heck of a lot better odds than the surety of dying in this side."

"Maybe we ease up on that trigger, Cap," Tai said, placing a hand on his shoulder. "Enough stuff out there trying to kill us, don't need something in here accidentally killing us."

He looked down. He had a tight, white knuckled grip on his side arm.

Zeph ran furious calculations through his console, muttering "We're all going to die," over and over to himself.

"We ain't dying yet." Dax said, balling his hands into fists and keeping them away from his thigh. "You know why?"

Zeph just shook his head, but Tai took the time to give him small smile.

"Why?" she asked.

"Because we owe people way too much money, and we ain't that lucky." Dax hit engage on the drivers. "Punch it Zeph!"

Their world turned into hues of fire red and electric blues while behind them a sun exploded.

CHAPTER 4

Dax always knew that death was going to catch up with him. Between the excessive gambling, the poor choices in company, and the rate at which the Kyrie went through her spare parts, and not so spare parts for that matter, he knew that he was bound to die sooner rather than later. He just didn't know that the rest of the galaxy would be hot on his heels.

The Kyrie folded space in front of itself. It wasn't ring travel, no faster than light physics here. But it was a really high coefficient of the speed of light, .845C to be exact. No, the Kyrie's Wedge drive simply folded the space in front of herself in the shape of a wedge that "pushed" matter out of the way.

It however did not work particularly well for any object close to or greater than Kyrie's mass. But then Dax was used to gambling with stakes that could cost a whole ship. Usually it was some solar system's variant of Texas Hold'em, but he figured he had better odds with blind intrasolar jumps then with cards: He owed a lot of money on bad card hands.

So it was with a quadruple chorus of sighs—Dax felt he could hear the ship herself exhale in relief—when they appeared, whole, and still alive, in space that resembled the Pica Solara major, the remaining twin star of the Pica system.

But that relief was short-lived.

"Where is…everything?" Tai said, pulling up her solar map, not that she would have forgotten the major details of a solar system on their route.

"We're all going to die," Zeph started repeating to himself again.

"I'm going hands-on, and try to bring us closer to the ring," Dax said. Without any better guide or data, he pointed the Kyrie in the general direction of the black albedo body against the sun and fired up the pulse engines.

"This isn't good," Tai said.

"I would think that with our entire galaxy wide communications being down, which by all accounts was supposed to be physically impossible, already made that an understatement." Dax was still hands-on, beginning the Kyrie on her half-hour deceleration to bring them closer to their destination.

"No, it's not that at all. Mamoru station isn't responding

to me."

"Tactum is down? No communications galaxy wide?" Dax gestured, taking in the entire screen in front of him. "We just talked about this."

"But the Mamoru should have redundancies upon redundancies for communication. Especially since it watches our side of the demilitarized zone with the People's Republic."

Tai was right. He had never gotten close to the two military installations, Mamoru, and its People's Republic counterpart Bohoja, without being hailed by countless 'This is a restricted zone. Cease or be fired upon' warnings. While the Pica system was firmly within the Cooperative's control, the rings were considered neutral space, since they could lead to any number of solar systems in the Galaxy, Cooperative, or Republic. It was why Pica was on their route in the first place.

But here he was, flying light seconds away from the two most fearsome and protected military installations in the system, with not a message or warning shot.

"Zeph, make sure we are pinging out our IFF signal anyway." He wanted to make sure the Mamoru identified the Kyrie as friend, not foe. It didn't hurt to be cautious.

Tai resumed her speech. "The Mamoru can withstand a nuclear attack. It can repel a whole fleet of supercarriers and destroyers. Even if something the size of a stellar container ship fell into its gravity well, it should survive. But that thing looks dead." Tai pointed to the highlighted installation.

Dax traced a square, bringing up the station in a magnified picture in picture view. While it was slightly distorted from zooming in, it did look like a badly damaged affair. The station was venting atmo from several fissures, and it was tilted on its side, not on the synchronous orbit it usually traveled around the Ring.

"Well here's to hoping that one of those redundancies doesn't decide to blast us out of the sky." The memory of the unnamed ship was still fresh in his mind. "Not only is the Mamoru the only reliable source of fuel left on this side of the solar system, we need to get past it to get out of this solar system." They had been scheduled to resupply on Pica 6, but he figured that wasn't really in the books anymore. Dax tapped his console, displaying the ships levels. They were low on virtually everything that the Kyrie could be low on.

They got within visual range of the Mamoru, her imposing visage visible from the portholes. Tiny drones that kept orbit around the station blinked in alternating colors, marking free and restricted zones in the surrounding space. Dax kept himself firmly in the green/white colored free zones.

Tai looked up from her console, which was scanning the base, to look at him. "You are still hands-on?"

"Voids yes. You know how hard it is to keep Kyrie in the lines using only retros?"

"That's isn't good either."

"I know, why does the military have to have such cramped

approach paths?"

"Because perimeter security should have stopped us before we even got close to the base and then T-drones would have been assigned to path us the rest of the way in."

Great. More bad news. He could feel the sweat on his hands and fingers, making the controls that much harder to maneuver, which in turn made him sweat more. His hands and fingers were cramping as well. He couldn't remember the last time he had been hands-on for such a contiguous period of time.

The Tactum had permeated all aspects of space life. Navigation, communication, virtually all facets of spacemanship had evolved since its discovery. He realized he had taken the presence of an instantaneous subspace communication link for granted. Everyone had, as far as he could tell, for the past hundreds of years since its discovery.

When the nature of one's world changed so fundamentally, how did one figure out their place in it?

"The world is going to be different now," he said, mostly to himself.

Zeph had his headset on, scanning through all frequencies for any signs of survivors, or barring that, maybe some sort of answer. But so far he had come back as twos and sevens. Hammers.

But Tai heard him, and she tilted her head quizzically and then, after a small moment of introspection, nodded gravely.

It was Tai's contemplative look. It was also her poker tell.

Tai was reserve Cooperative Navy, and he was retired Cooperative Marines. Together they made a great team. The Kyrie wasn't a drop ship, and her crew wasn't a marine strike force, but at least he didn't have a boss, and he wasn't forced to shoot as many people. Some, just not as much.

She looked down on her console. "It might be a tight fit, but there is a small crafts dock coming up. Do you think you are going to have a problem maneuvering the Kyrie into it?"

They rounded a corner of the station. Dax grimaced. "No Tai, I don't think it's going to be any problem at all," he said, nodding to the gaping maw of ablated metal, scorched ceramic, and exposed structural beams.

Tai stood from her console, peered out of the nearest porthole to confirm, and then walked to view screen, taking in the scene of destruction presented before her.

"This isn't good at all."

CHAPTER 5

Dax could see from the debris and the general shape of the remaining structure that this had been an implosion and not an explosion. Something strong and something powerful had punched into the Mamoru's armored sides. In fact, now that they were on the side that faced the ring, it was clear that this was not the only, nor even the largest, of such areas of damage.

"What could have done that?" Tai stood there, motionless. As a reservist, she would have known many spacers stationed here.

"Don't know, but I don't want to be here if it returns, yeah?" Dax carefully maneuvered into the exposed space, smaller debris being pushed away by the Kyrie's hull. He even had to angle her nose slightly down to match with the ruined floor. "Zeph, we getting any artificial grav?"

"Negative boss." Zeph replied. "From what I can tell, the Mamoru is on a quickly deteriorating orbit that is eventually going to impact with the Ring. And it's a little hard to tell because of the scale, but the base has fractured, and the segment we're on is on an uncontrolled lateral spin."

"Give me a threat analysis if I park her here using just mags?"

"I wouldn't suggest it for the long term. Between the aforementioned deteriorating orbit and the chance of this part of the base just shearing off from the main structure, I'm guessing we only got about an hour or two."

In and out as fast as he could. Like a sketchy poker game in the bad part of town. "You grab the pot and I'll punch them out." He turned to Tai, who was, as usual, two steps ahead of him. She was already in her skin tight bodysuit that would go underneath their EVA gear. She was also armed. Well, he wasn't going to disagree with her caution. "Zeph, man the ship, keep scanning for external signatures, but also watch our backs. Active pings, and also keep broadcasting that IFF. I don't feel like getting shot today, all right?"

"All right." Zeph put his game face on.

"I mean it. Can't afford to patch up another EVA suit again. Heck, forget about the money, maintaining these suits is a life or death situation now."

Zeph just touched his two fingers to his brow in the barest of salutes. His hands were already flying through his console, having pulled up Tai's screen and docked it to his own. He was one of the few people Dax knew that could handle two command consoles at once. When someone brought it up though, Zeph would just shrug and blame video games.

With a little love tap, Dax brought the Kyrie in-line with the deck and as free as possible from floating debris. "Engaging mag locks," he said as way of warning, but both Zeph and Tai were stowed away. There was a slight gut-wrenching lift from his frame of gravity as the magnetic docking legs of the Kyrie pulled the rest of the ship downwards towards the deck, making strong contact.

He gave Zeph a thumbs-up as he left the command bay, but Zeph was firmly engrossed monitoring his two consoles. He closed the airlock behind him. A short walk past their cabins, and another airlock, and he was in the cargo bay, where Tai was already partway into her suit. He helped her get most of the hard-to-attach segments on, and then turned to change into his suit, with Tai returning the favor.

He pressed on a small blister on the outside of his wristcom. "Zeph, we're geared up. Open up the cargo bay doors on my mark."

"I'm sorry Dax, but I can't do that."

Tai grimaced in her helmet. "Now that is an ancient cinema reference. Weren't they still using film then to watch things?"

Dax laughed. "And burning fossil fuels. It seemed

appropriate, considering our utterly prehistoric circumstances!" Space Odyssey 2001 had been very advanced for its time, but was already an outdated vision of space when 2001 had eventually rolled around. It was prehistoric by today's standards. But that generation of spacers had cobbled together some crude and ancient form of space travel, both in their fiction and in real life, all without the Tactum. If they could do it back then, they could do it now.

He was snapped out of his reverie by a friendly tap on his visor. "You got a little thousand yard stare there, Cap."

He shook himself. "Sorry, Yup. Okay, we gotta be fast and we gotta be concise. We need scrubber to breathe, filters to drink, cells to fly, 'topes to jump—"

"And cartridges to shoot," Tai said, pulling back on the charging handle of her sub compact.

"You're right. Seeing as there ain't really nobody left to enforce the restrictions on our Class C transport license."

"Not that it stopped us before," Tai said. She smiled.

"Zeph?" Dax didn't hear a reply except the hiss of the cargo bay air lock cycling, the oxygen pressure rapidly dropping as most of it rushed out to fill the empty space of the dock and even slowly escape into space.

The scene of utter destruction presented before him took his breath away. But thankfully, not literally. His suit was pumping pressurized air into a helmet to maintain a solid one atmospheric pressure environment. The suit was so simple that the loss of the Tactum only disabled the auto designate overlays on Dax's visor, replaced instead with a small "signal loss" warning in the bottom right of his HUD.

A small, innocuous yet ominous reminder that the world had been altered beyond recognition a few hours past.

He scrunched the toes on his right foot, releasing the magnet, and took a step down the bay ramp. Then relaxed his toes to reengage the small mag locks on his suit's boot soles. Same with the left foot. Scrunch, drag, relax. Scrunch, drag, relax. For a few minutes he was lost in the rhythm and the physicality of it all.

But then he stopped and looked up, but in zero gravity, up was really arbitrary. Everything had gone dark. It was like he was looking up into a bottomless well of inky blackness. And then he was wasn't look up anymore but rather he was hanging upside-down over a charcoal black pit, and if he let go, it would swallow him up whole and not even notice he was missing.

There was a tap on his faceplate. Tai was looking at him, slight concern in her eyes. She waved her hand over her face, and then pointed two fingers at his eyes then hers: "You in there?"

Dax swallowed once, and then took too deep of a breath, the drastic change in pressure creating a familiar sharp pain in his eyes. Even breaths. In, then out. He focused on the pain, bringing himself back into the now.

He tapped twice on his helmet, and then gave Tai a thumbs-up, an apologetic grin plastered on his face, large enough for Tai to see through the helmet: "Head case. But I'm okay now."

He stepped away from the maw of the dark universe trying to swallow him up.

CHAPTER 6

Soon enough, Tai and he were at the mouth of the airlocks that would lead into the base's interior. When he turned to look at Tai, she was intently staring at a holo of the base's map. "I'm seeing a storage and supply hold a little ways in and a few levels down."

"Well, let's hope it's intact, unlike this deck." He waved in the general direction of the mayhem behind him. There was a lot of debris, and even some figures that could have been empty suits. The helmets had fogged over so he couldn't see inside to verify if they were empty or not. He was trying really hard to not go through the logical chain implying that if the helmet visors had fogged up, then there had been a person in there to provide moisture to condense on the inside.

Zeph's voice came in like a tight buzz, not able to use the Tactum to piggyback the audio signal and using the Kyrie's antenna instead. "I am getting LOS on all diagnostic sensors inside the deck. I can't even tell if there is any pressure or artgrav in there. So just be careful. Use suit sensors."

Dax exhaled, misting his visor in the process. Don't think about fogged up helmets. Voids. Some lights were flickering, those that hadn't just been crushed by the violent depressurization. Most were some sort of emergency lights that cast an eerie glow. But even if the docking bay had been fully lit up, he still would have felt blind.

He didn't know what lay beyond these doors. He turned to Tai, whose face was framed by floating strands of black hair that had escaped her hasty buns and her determined set glare.

"Ready?" he said, hitting the transmit blister.

She just nodded and gave him a thumbs-up without looking at him. They split, taking cover from either side of the door well, and crouched. Tai had her subcompact firmly pressed against her shoulder and trained at eye level around her corner. Dax took a firm grip of his sidearm on his right hand and then, with a slight moment of hesitation, released the airlock.

Clear. Another quick nod to Tai and then he was carefully going through the airlock, gun in front of him. The dark cavern that was the base's interior swallowed him up in blackness.

Six lights pierced the inky blackness. The light from his sidearm and Tai's sub and a pair of lights from each of their respective EVA suit helmets. Dax would have preferred to bring even more, to fight back against the oppressive darkness.

But soon his eyes adjusted and it became less a house of terror, if only slightly so. The random floating objects and even some body parts, however, did not help.

Tai tapped on his helmet and gave him the hand signal to ask if he was okay. He took a deep breath and then flashed her the thumbs-up, follow by the "so-so" signal.

She patted him on the shoulder and then pointed to her eyes, and then down the dark corridor. Eyes up, on the move.

He nodded and assumed the position behind Tai as she took point. Their progress was slow but determined, the mag locks on their boots marking their path in rhythmic scraping. Every few turns, Dax would drop a bright green glow stick, marking their path back to the Kyrie. And once in a while, Tai would make a sweeping motion, and Dax would assume point while Tai conferred with her holo map.

Tai's voice came over the intercom. "There is an airlock into the next block around the corner. I'm getting atmo and thermal bleed signatures, which is promising."

He nodded, and with a tap from Tai on the shoulder, he rounded the corner.

And he collided with a figure in an EVA suit. At such a close distance, Dax opted to bring up his shoulder instead of his weapon. He rammed into the body in front of him, pinned it against the wall, and then brought up his sidearm, about to pistol-whip his opponent in the face.

At which point he realized that the suit he had pinned against the wall housed a dead spacer.

With a shudder he let the figure drop and then pulled away. Tai came in closer to inspect the body.

"Her 02 is still at 60%, so it must have been something else that got her." She turned the body over. "Ah, shrapnel of some sort. Looks like she died from internal bleeding."

Dax nodded and gulped, not trusting his voice. Tai pulled the body to the side, and then took position next to the door. She placed a hand on the exterior lock. She pushed once on the wheel, getting it started, pushed it a few more times, and then spun it the rest of the way. There was a minor decompression, the airlock having a little bit of atmo left from the last transfer. Dax closed the external lock and gave Tai the thumbs-up, signaling for her to start pumping atmosphere into the lock.

Tai kept her eyes glued on the panel, occasionally glancing at her wristcom to confirm the panel's readouts. She gave the thumbs-up back to Dax when the target pressure had been reached.

He took position on the opposite side of the door, ready to rush in the moment Tai released the airlock. She pulled on the interior lock until it hit hard left. With a silent three count that Dax read from her breathing, she yanked the door open, and Dax advanced with the sidearm raised, sweeping the dimly lit cabin. A few heartbeats later, Tai rushed in, taking position on his right shoulder.

"Clear," Tai said.

"Clear," Dax said in agreement, and they both brought their guns down, While Tai checked sensors, Dax tried to get Zeph and the Kyrie on comms.

"Zeph, can you read me?" He let go of the blister, waiting for a response. "Nothing."

"We're too far into the hull of the base. The radio won't reach," Tai said, knocking on the durasteel superstructure

"Not having the Tactum is going to take some getting used to." Dax shook his head.

"Good news", Tai said, looking up from her wristcom, "we've got atmo pressure and breathable oxygen in here."

"Thank goodness for tiny miracles."

Tai nodded in agreement, and took off her helmet.

Dax followed suit, gulping, and then disciplined himself to let out a controlled exhale before removing his helmet. He took a breath. The air had the staleness of recycled air and traces of mechanic grease. It brought him back to his time on the OCSS Peregrine as a marine. His sergeant had always said that Cooperative space stations ran on recycled blood, sweat, and tears.

Of course, this Cooperative station wasn't going to be recycling much of anything any time soon.

He took a few steadying breaths, making sure to equalize

himself in this new pressure environment. The controlled breathing also helped him calm down.

Of course that was all in vain when he felt a cold muzzle pressed against his skull.

"Don't move," the voice attached to the muzzle said.

CHAPTER 7

"Ease up on the firearm, friend," a voice intoned. She, it was definitely a she, had a distinct colonial accent to it. Maybe from one of the Pacificka colonies, Dax figured.

Tai was already whipping around and drawing her subcompact, but another figure with a cold barrel pointed his gun at Tai.

"You are quick, but focused on the wrong threat, yaar," said a second figure

Dax saw Tai round on the figure, about to go after the small man pointing a gun at her face, consequences be void.

"And by the wrong threat, my brother meant me." A third figure, this one wielding a rifle, appeared. Three hostiles, one more than ten feet away from Tai. Tai was fast, but not that fast.

"Now my men and I are willing to deescalate hostilities," the first voice said, "if you promise that neither of you are going to start shooting up the place."

Dax looked Tai square in the eye. No need for heroics. She rolled her eyes and lowered her weapon nonchalantly, as if she didn't have two weapons pointed directly at her.

The woman attached to the voice, who Dax assumed was in command, had already lowered hers and Dax had not been fast enough to draw his sidearm from his holster but he did pull his hands away from his waist in a conciliatory gesture.

"No shooting. I'm actually aiming to not get shot, if at all possible. See, Tai wagered some money on the fact that I can't ever seem to leave the ship without riling someone up enough to launch ammunition at me."

The woman in command nodded, and he could see a smile at the edge of her lips. "Now why would someone do that, seeing as you are a reasonable sort of fella?" Dax was trying to place the pleasant, almost seductive accent. Australian colonies? Close but not quite.

"That's what I say!" He turned to Tai. "Didn't I just say on Pica 6 that they wouldn't be shooting at me if they just knew how nice a fella I am?"

"Very much so, sir. But I do recall extenuating circumstances." Tai relaxed a fraction.

"Them being?"

"Them being that they had just caught you cheating at the card table."

Oh yeah. That was true. Dax laughed at himself. "Well,

still, it was mighty rude of them to start shooting." He looked at the Cooperative marine's rank insignia. "Well, Sergeant 'Ramirez,' you aren't planning on being rude and start shooting, are you?"

Ramirez looked from him to Tai, and then at him again. Then she smiled. "Weapons down, boys." She made the same conciliatory gesture, hands away from the hips.

The two other Cooperative marines followed suit and without their rifles in front of their face, it was obvious that they were, if not brothers, close relatives. They went to their sergeant and took flanking positions on either side of her.

Dax approached the marines, Tai in tow. He extended a hand. "Daxton McCloud, freelance transporter. This is my second, Tatsu Hanamura."

"Sergeant Theresa Ramirez," she took his hand, "Our Cooperative Marine Corps."

The two marines on her side approached. The one with just a mustache waved. "Abe, nice to meet ya."

The second also waved, but this one with a bigger smile. "Far, pleasure." He said that second part with a wink towards Tai, who just coolly raised her eyebrow.

Dax felt the threat of imminent danger leave his chest. "Glad that didn't turn ugly."

"Like his mom," Abe said, jerking a thumb at Far. Far gave a rude gesture in return.

Ramirez shook her head. "The Rahmani brothers,

Abrahim and Farrhid. But we usually just call them idiots."

The two brothers grinned.

"It's because our mother dropped him when he was younger," Far said, coming in to conspiratorially whisper behind his hand in a loud voice.

"Only so that you wouldn't feel intimidated," Abe said, with the same conspiratorial whisper behind the hand, on Dax's other side.

It had the feel of a rehearsed bit. Hilarious. "You two ever think about retiring and taking this act on the road?"

"Alas," Far said, pausing for a little dramatic tension, "my brother here can only survive in an environment where he is constantly being given clear and concise orders. I fear he would not manage to tie his own boots if he were not commanded to be dressed at revelry."

Abe mimed strangling Far, and just smiled.

"Both of you are hopeless. And the poorest excuses for marines this side of the galaxy." Ramirez said it in a way which made it clear that she was endeared, if slightly annoyed by the two's antics. "So, freelance transporter, that means—"

Dax raised his hands. "Now before you start, there actually is a huge swath of difference between me and a pirate. For one, I don't have a skull on my flag. And two, no peg leg."

Ramirez was unperturbed by his outburst. "That means you have a ship then?"

He could feel the heat rising on his cheeks. "Oh, yes, her

name is Kyrie. We have her docked nearby. We just offloaded our shipment on Pica 3 and we were going to resupply on Pica 6, but then the end of the world happened."

"The external small crafts dock, I assume. The nearest one in this sector, four decks below?"

"Well, there aren't really decks anymore as much as remains of what used to be decks. What would you say Tai?" he turned to his second.

"There could have been four decks worth of destruction below us." Tai had resumed her stoic position of arms crossed and legs shoulder width apart, serious expression on her face, her long straight black hair cutting a severe profile. "But marine, how did this happen? How do two orbital defense platforms just get destroyed?"

"You don't know?" Ramirez's face went from dark to horror. "But you were at an external cargo dock, how could you not?"

Dax grimaced a bit. "Well, see, we were actually at the other side of the solar system, you know, before the second sun exploded."

Ramirez nodded. "I could only assume it was also bad in the other parts of the system. But when we lost station wide communications, we assumed the worst. A People's Republic surprise attack, or some radiological weapon we weren't prepared for. But then the missiles started firing, and the nightmare became real."

CHAPTER 8

"Missiles? Why didn't the station deploy point defenses?" Tai's voice was almost accusatory, as if she was holding Ramirez personally liable.

"No, you don't understand. Missiles from both sides. Ours and theirs."

Dax held up his hand to forestall Tai. "Let Sergeant Ramirez explain. We aren't going to get anywhere with you interrupting her."

Ramirez nodded and then took a deep breath.

"You both seem to have some basic understanding of our military deployment and organization here in Pica system, but there is a lot about these stations that isn't known to even the well-informed civilian." She pulled up her wristcom and scanned through it, finally bringing up a small holo of 2 large objects orbiting a third.

"Both stations, the Mamoru and Bohoja, aren't just your typical military orbital station; they are officially classified as orbital standoff weapon platforms. It's even in their names. Mamoru is Cooperative standard for "to protect", while Bohoja is Republican for "guardian."

"OSWPs are designed for redundancies. Besides the expected complement of weapons, point defenses, and shield arrays, there is auto-targeting anti-space perimeter weapons set to lock onto targets marked as foe in space. Then there are reactive defense weapons, in a smaller perimeter, set to lock onto targets not marked as friendly in space. That's why drones have to bring you into the base docking bays." She paused. "Used to, anyway."

Ramirez's face looked crestfallen, but before Dax could prompt her to go on she took a sharp breath and continued. "And then the standoff weapons. Long-range radiological and anti-material weaponry. Some were set to go off if a stand-down code isn't entered in periodically. A large number of weapons officers on this station spend most of their day just reentering stand-down codes. And then there are dead man switch standoff weapons. Weapons set to go off the moment the bases' critical systems go down."

"Such as?" Tai asked. At this point she was completely enraptured by the sergeant's description of the bases. She was eating it up.

"Life support. Comms. The weapon's platform itself,

ironically. Shields and Identity Friend or Foe targeting."

"Makes sense," Dax said. "So what happened?"

"A complete comet foxtrot happened."

"Comet foxtrot?"

"Cluster fu—"

"Okay okay, I get it." That one had not been popular with his previous unit. "But, I mean, what exactly happened?"

"The moment the Tactum went down, some of the dead man switch defenses automatically assumed the worst and started shooting."

Tai interrupted. "Shooting what?"

Ramirez leaned back against the scaffolding of the cabin. Not at rest, just a soldier at ease. Still dangerous, still serious. At her nonverbal command, the Rahmani brothers took their ease as well and Dax noticed for the first time that all three of them carried extra gear.

She continued. "At first they just shot at their predetermined targets. The Cooperative's backup plan was always to, if not protect the Ring, deny it from Republic control. The first volley launched straight at the Bohoja.

"Then the Bohoja started firing. Whether in response to our attack, or as a result of their own dead man switches, we don't know. Might never know. We fired, they fired, we returned fire, they returned fire."

"With the Tactum down, the Identity Friend and Foe, IFF system was down. There was a carrier station in this system.

"I'm pretty sure the Mamoru sent a bit of ordinance her way. Of the Wedge drive variety."

Dax contemplated the story. "There wasn't a way to just, you know, stop? Maybe even surrender?"

Abe shook his head. "We tried, yaar. We did. And that was no simple feat with the Tactum down. We tried tight beam, long wave, shortwave, by Allah, we sent Morse code."

"And none of it went through?"

"Of course it went through! We're only a few light seconds away." Abe sighed. "There were protocols in place, obviously, for this exact situation. Accidental discharge of weaponry, a de-escalation and stand down procedure."

Far stepped in, patting his brother on the back. "It was the protocols that eventually screwed us. Our junior signal officer reached one of their junior signal officers. He demanded authentication codes before he could proceed, before he'd even listen to us. And with the Tactum down, we had to run down the codes manually, using handhelds and paper. The codes are only good for five minutes before they expire!"

Abe and Ramirez raised their eyebrows in agreement, as if they were relieving the experience themselves. Far continued. "The junior signal officer finally gets her superior officer on the horn. He demands more authentication, all the while our two stations are trying to destroy each other and every large object in the system. All the while our codes are expiring every five damn minutes!"

Ramirez spread her arms. "We don't even know if we ever got word to someone who could make a decision. Maybe we did, but maybe that person got killed, or maybe he faced the same problems we had. We were trying to hook up some sort of rudimentary Friend or Foe system to speak with the targeting telemetry. Wires! We were trying to network them using wires, for void's sake. It's like we were back in the Stone Age."

"We finally were able to set up enough ad hoc replacement systems, and just disable the rest, but there was always something we had missed, always something that either the Tactum had always taken care of before or else someone that was now dead only knew how to fix. One destroyer that was stationed here tried to send docking pods to offer assistance." Ramirez exhaled and then slumped. "Maybe the Mamoru thought they were missiles? Shot all the pods down, pods full of people just trying to help the station. Then it auto targeted the 'threat' with standoff weapons. The destroyer was spooling up her jump jets last I saw, before something took out our visual scanners."

Dax folded his arms. "I'm sorry for your losses, sergeant. It's pretty bad out there too." He paused. "Look, normally I'd wait an appropriate time, maybe a moment of silence, before pressuring you, but this ain't normal out there. We need to resupply our ship and get out of here right quick. I noticed you folks have some gear stowed already?"

"We have a good bit, yes. Cooperative protocol is to scuttle this station to prevent it from falling into enemy hands. Lots of sensitive material and tech in here. That's why I'm glad you have a ship. I thought we were going to have to—" Dax read a whole galaxy's worth of unfinished sentences in that brief pause. "Well, let's just say I'm glad to be able to give a go at surviving a bit more."

"You're welcome to join us. We could use the company, that's for sure. But we also need a few components for our ship, and fuel."

"That's going to be a bit tricky. One of the last systems ad hoc'd to our Frankenstein standoff network was a blank slate Friend and Foe targeting matrix. We don't know exactly what the parameters are, but we've been locked out of a lot of decks and armories. We could cut our way through," Ramirez gestured to Abe who lifted up a torch, "but it's very time-consuming. And I didn't need your story to know that time is in short supply."

Tai's radio squawked at that point. "I think I can help with that, Captain," Zeph's voice said over the radio.

CHAPTER 9

"I actually got the idea while I was listening to Ramirez's story," Zeph said, still over the radio.

"You were able to listen in on us?" Tai asked. "How? We lost signal several decks ago."

"I think one of your marines is carrying a signal repeater?"

Abe raised his hand sheepishly. "Guilty. It's the only way we can communicate in here. And we weren't really worried about being listened in on, since we were basically looking for anybody that was still alive at this point. No dice."

"Anyway, you were broadcasting in the clear, and I started listening in. It was only when I heard you two responding that I realized that I had picked up someone in your vicinity, Captain."

Dax grabbed the set from Tai. "Okay, but you said something about helping. We should get to helping before these two bases get to firing."

Ramirez got his attention. "I assume this voice is a member of your crew?"

"Our astrogator, Zeph," Dax said.

"At your service. Now the problem here, as I reckon it, is the IFF database isn't recognizing you as part of their system."

"Affirmative," Ramirez said

"Secondary issues here, the Friend database is encrypted. Now, I could typically break into this encryption right quick, but I don't have access to my tools on the cloud." Zeph took a breath. "I guess there isn't a cloud anymore. I spent ten years programming those tools, and now they're gone."

Tai grabbed the radio from Dax. "Focus."

"Of course of course of course." Dax could almost hear Zeph shaking himself. "So we can't dump your IDs into the Friend database, but what I can do is create a new directory and grant that directory elevated privileges within the base.

Ramirez approached the radio. "Is that really going to work?"

"If Zeph says it," Dax said, "it usually works out like he says it will. He's good like that."

"Thanks boss man," Zeph said over the radio.

"Don't get too cocky, though." Dax dropped his voice. "You sure about this kid? If you are wrong, we could end up a bit dead."

"I'm looking at the based network heuristics. What

Ramirez said was true: they really just tried to cobble the most rudimentary IFF system in here. Sure, that one database is encrypted, but there is hardly any security on any of the other systems. Cakewalk."

"All right, what do you need?"

"I need everyone's ID tags synced to yours."

Dax nodded, even though he knew Zeph couldn't see. He held out his wristcom. "Sync up, boys and girls."

Tai proffered her wrist, and her gold ID tag appeared above her wrist, and then was transferred to Dax's. Ramirez, as a commanding officer of her squad, flicked her wrist, and a que of five ID tags appeared above hers, all emerald indicating Cooperative Military.

"Five?" Dax asked.

"I got my heavy weapons specialist and my newbie in an adjacent corridor doing sweeps. Which reminds me." She keyed in the radio set on her helmet. "Mbikala, Kelly, to me."

Two "rogers" could be heard faintly. A few moments later, the door adjacent to the one that Tai and Dax had first entered in opened and a large Black man and a diminutive Caucasian girl came in.

They both saluted Ramirez. "Introduce yourselves to our new friends, and possibly saviors," she said.

"Specialist Jean-Gerard Mbikala, Kingdom of Congo colonies, guns," the tall shaved headed man said in a deep, smokey voice. He shifted his large machine gun to his shoulder and offered the freed hand. "My friends call me 'Bik.'"

"Rochelle Kelly, Private homegrown in the UC of A." United Colonies of America. Blond and blue-eyed, Kelly sounded rural and perky. "They call me 'Newbie,'" she said, almost petulantly, before grinning. "But, I guess, not undeserved." The two introduced themselves to Tai.

"And I already introduced you to the Rahmani brothers, of course," Ramirez said, and the two brothers perked up and waved, in opposite identical gestures.

"PFC Abrahim Rahmani, signal intelligence."

"Private First Class Farrid Rahmani, drone ops." He paused. "I'm kinda useless now."

"Now?" His brother said. "Try always."

Ramirez interrupted them with a raised hand. "But I guess I forget to introduce myself. Theresa Ramirez, Aotearoa Kingdom colonies."

"Aotearoa," Dax worked the word around in his mouth. "That used to be New Zealand, correct? I knew I recognized the accent!"

"Actually, if we are being pedantic, New Zealand used to be, and is once again, the Kingdom of Aotearoa. The land of White clouds. And you?"

"The last name didn't give it away? United Kingdom colonies, Clan McCloud."

"Tai Nakamura, Cooperative central colonies." Tai bowed

slightly to Ramirez and her squad.

"Ohayō gozaimasu," Bik said, returning her slight bow.

"What he said." Abe pointed a thumb over his shoulder at Bik. "And salaam, of course." Far and Abe bowed slightly their hands over their hearts.

Ramirez took a closer look at Tai. "Nakamura. Not the Inner Systems—"

Dax intervened. "We don't like to talk about that."

She considered, and then nodded.

"Well that was all heartwarming and all, and while you all were forgetting to introduce me to the party, I was busy embedding a database that's gonna save all y'all's butts."

"And that is our astrogator, Zeph, born and raised in 'nobody knows,' colony of 'nobody cares.'"

"I've never heard the Canadian colonies described so accurately." There was a moment of silence, and then Dax's wristcom holo came to life, displaying an internal map of the Mamoru. "In other news, I just saved our lives, if you all could just kindly grab the parts and supplies we need to get off this death trap of a space station." Two red paths were superimposed over the map. "If ya don't mind."

"You heard the polite Canadian gentleman," Dax said, hefting his gear bag. "Let's loot the solar system's most formidable military installation."

CHAPTER 10

They ended up splitting into two teams to more efficiently grab the essential parts for the Kyrie. Only Tai and Dax could speak directly with Zeph, while all the marines could speak with each other over their shortwave radios, so Tai attached herself to Ramirez and Bik, while Dax went along with the Rahmani brothers and Kelley.

"Don't skimp on the O2 scrubbers," Dax said to Tai, before they split up.

"Thanks for the reminder, Captain. For I surely would have not remembered how important breathable oxygen was to our survival. Feel free to remember not to skimp on the fuel cells that drive all essential systems of our ship."

And in characteristic Tai fashion, she was off.

A few minutes into their separate ways, Dax found himself behind the Rahmani brothers cracking more "your mother" jokes. He turned to Kelley. "Okay, so how do you tell them apart without looking at their badges?"

"Oh that's easy," Kelley said, a smirk on her face. She leaned in as if she was about to share some salacious gossip. "Far is always wearing his tactical scarf, while Abe often does not. I think the sergeant might have ordered them to dress differently back when they first joined, and they opted on that."

"Actually," Far said, bringing Dax up short before he ran into the two suddenly stopped brothers, "it is called a shemagh."

"Hardly," Abe said. "My dear brother would like you to believe that his flamboyant red accessory is a masculine article, but it is clear that it is in fact a keffiyeh, a woman's scarf."

"You only wish you were masculine enough to be able to wear such a beautiful art piece." Far pretended to scoff his brother and turned back.

"If only your mother had been able to impart some level of fashion sense to you, before abandoning you, she would have done us all a favor."

The forced levity helped lighten the mood as they made their way down the dark passageways. The black was broken only by the intermittent emergency light and the beams from the muzzles of the marines' weapons.

Far rotated with Kelly as rearguard and Abe took point.

Far whispered to Dax, "if you really want to know, I, Farrid Rahmani, am the better looking of the pair. Abe takes too much after his mother." Again, more ribs at their absent biological parent. It was probably a sensitive subject for the two, which naturally led to them constantly joking about it.

Abe raised a fist, calling a halt, and then referenced his wristcom. "Supply and arms depot B17 should be just around the corner."

They turned the corner and an armor reinforced door appeared. "Let's see if your boy Zeph did his magic." Abe waved his wristcom over the panel. Dax held his breath. They needed what was behind these doors in a really bad way. For one moment nothing happened, then the reader blinked green, and with a hiss the door retracted, the room behind it equalizing in pressure with their surroundings.

They walked in, and it felt like he had just been handed the last card for a flush on the turn. It was a smuggler's paradise. And Dax would know. He considered himself only one step, and sometimes less, above a smuggler. There were guns. Lots of military grade weapons lined the shelves of the bare steel walls. Weapons that would sell well on the black-market. If that still existed. And explosives of all shapes and sizes. Beacon transmitters. Meals ready-to-eat. Nano-block munitions. And of course, sweet sweet fuel cells.

While larger ships, and most likely this station, ran on large antimatter reactors, smaller ships used the more portable

PFCs. Which was lucky for them, because while an AMR was small, it was dense. Easy to transport.

Dax cleaned out the entire depot's supply of large cells, the kind that would fit the Kyrie's main reactor, and then took a few of the medium and small cells for good measure. Other vehicles and devices could use the universal power sources, including the marine's energy weaponry.

The marines were loading up on other sundry supplies as well as additional arms and ammunition. Dax understood the compulsion well. Abe was loading a few beacons as well. "It's the only reliable way to transmit a strong signal remotely with the Tactum gone," he said with a shrug. Golden rule about communications: If the radio operator said the equipment was necessary, it was necessary.

He picked up a large designated marksmen rifle, a beautiful semi-automatic large caliber beauty with accessories that would sync with his wristcom.

"Now officially," Far said, sneaking up behind Dax, "I'm supposed to tell you that it's a capital felony to commandeer Cooperative Military equipment." Far smiled, and there was a mischievous twinkle in his eye. "But seeing as it's the end of the world and all, I figured I can turn a blind eye. Just this once."

"How kind of you, seeing as we are only going to save your life in return."

"Oh, it's nothing. Don't sweat the small things." He

turned to the shelf next to Dax, and his face lit up. "Ooh, portable missile launchers. Gimme gimme."

Across the room, Kelly was shouldering a sniping platform weapon system and then stuffing magazines of its anti-materiel rounds into her bag.

Ramirez's voice came over Far's radio set. "Now don't you all get greedy on me. Remember, we have limited time and space. Grab the essentials and then Oscar Mike your way to our RZ." The rendezvous point was the room they had first met, barring any better choices. "Don't forget, the Bohoja could start spinning up any time it feels like."

At the mention of the Bohoja's point defense weapons, Dax could see a shiver run through all three marines. It must have been a nightmare, sitting inside a space station, watching ordinance the size of small vehicles magnetically accelerated through space, and being able to do nothing to defend yourself.

"We're just finishing up here, Sarge," Far said, keying the radio receiver. "We're thirty-five minutes out."

"Stay frosty, Far. Over and out."

And like that, their illicit shopping spree was at an end. Dax could have almost cried a tear. He looked at walls lined with thousands upon thousands of efforts worth of military equipment. Oh well, there were probably very few people he still owed money to left in this galaxy. There was a silver lining to the end of the world.

CHAPTER 11

Dax's team rejoined with Tai's, both parties laden with large sacks, as well as pushing carts and hand trucks loaded with supplies.

"It's like a postapocalyptic Christmas!" Abe said.

"Yes," Dax said, "All I want for Christmas is to survive."

Several of them nodded and Bik even did so reverently. He then looked to Kelly. "Were you able to find it?"

"Barely, big guy," Kelly said while she reached into her duffel. "This is one serious mother." She pulled out the meanest machine railgun Dax had ever seen.

The large man broke into smile and easily hefted the beast with one hand, using his other hand to inspect the weapon.

"You just couldn't resist, huh?" Ramirez said.

Bik at least had the sense to pretend to blush. "If we are going to face the end of the world, sergeant, I would like to do so well armed."

"And you two?" looking at the Rahmani brothers. Abe pulled out a kinetic shotgun, while Far hefted a very formidable grenade launcher.

Ramirez covered her face with a gloved hand and turned to Kelly. "Do I even want to know?"

"Well, Sarge, as you know, when I got into the Corp, I was really hankering to be . . ." She pulled out the large sniper rifle Dax had seen her eying earlier.

Ramirez just sat there, arms on her hips. She looked sternly at all four of her subordinates. "Well?" she said, looking about to say something severe. "What did you get me?"

Her squad broke into a grin, and the Rahmani brothers step together to block her view, as Kelly grabbed something from the bag. They split apart at a tap from Kelly, and she presented the sergeant with a steel beauty. It looked like an old-fashioned revolver, but it was really a miniaturized linear mass accelerator.

Ramirez lifted the "revolver" gently, almost reverently, turning it over in her hands.

"Just like the one you lost in—" Kelly began.

Bik put his hand on Kelly's shoulder. "Let's not ruin the moment."

Tai cut into their reverie. "This is all really touching, but let us not forget, mendokusai, that this station is on a decomposing orbit towards the Ring itself. Not to mention that it or its counterpart might start firing at any moment."

"She might start firing at any moment," Ramirez said, while rubbing a hand at her cheek. Where those tears?

"Yes, yes, I am Reserve Cooperative Navy. I am familiar with the pedantries." Cooperative ships and space installations where always "she," while Republican ships and space installations where designated "he."

"We've got a problem, folks." Zeph's voice came over Tai and Dax's coms, and the marine squad's radios.

"I know, I just said decomposing orbit and standoff—"

"No, bigger."

"Bigger than being destroyed by a gravity well or tactical radiological weapons?" Dax's fingers were sweating again, as he pressed on the blister on his wristcom to transmute.

"Okay," Zeph said, "let me correct myself. It is a bigger immediate threat."

Ramirez spoke sternly into her should radio, interrupting Dax and Zeph. "All right astrogator, spit it out."

"All I know is the Friend or Foe Indicator is labeling them as 'Anti-Personnel Hunter Killer Drones.' They don't sound friendly and they're heading your way."

Far swore. "Comet Foxtrot!"

"Anti-Personnel Drones," Dax said. "I know what those are." Just by the definition of the words that made up the name, they were robots designed to kill people. "But I have no clue what 'hunter killer' implies."

"It's pretty straightforward." Far pulled up a holo on his wrist screen. "It means they actively pursue their programmed targets through a cascading threat and opportunity algorithm." Great, killer robots that learned how to kill better.

"But they still should be programmed, right?" Kelley asked. "I thought you added us as friendly in the IFF." She spoke this into Dax's comm, directed at Zeph.

"Not really, I added you as an elevated user group in the IFF, because the folder was corrupted. I'm trying now, to get you assigned as Friend for the drone protocols, but I'm getting blocked."

"No," Far said, scrolling through lines of code on his wristcom. "It is not your fault, Astrogator Zeph." He turned to the rest of the squad. "The drones IFF protocol is master key locked. They were designed, ironically enough, for a situation like this, if the Republic was ever able to invade the Mamoru and interrupt the Identity protocol. The drones actively seek targets not authenticated against the main profile and . . ."

"And the main profile is corrupted," Zeph finished.

"Hammers," Dax said, pulling his side arm and checking the charge on the weapon. He grabbed some of the universal charge clips and docked the first into the weapon and a few more on his bandoleer. "It's always hammers, isn't it? Every hand we've been dealt since the Tactum fell has been hammers."

"Wha—" Ramirez said, before Tai placed a hand on her arm.

"Dax loses a lot of money in Centauri Hold'em." Tai started loading her sub-compact. "A lot of money."

Ramirez and her squad were professionals. They were likewise checking their charges and arming up. Bik was spinning up his Gatling railgun, and the sound was formidable.

"Locked and loaded, Sarge," Far said.

"Okay, we're Oscar Mike, folks." Ramirez followed her own advice, picking up her weapon. She was operational and mobile.

Mobile, only by the laxest definition. They were carrying kilos of armaments and supplies, and yes, they were moving. Moving very slowly.

Zeph noticed. "Guys, you all really need to haul behind. If these readings are correct, they are gaining on you, fast."

"Astrogator, we are moving as quickly as possible, I assure you," Abe said, locking the previous airlock behind him after they all moved through it.

They were dead if they abandoned the supplies. They were dead if they stayed with them. "It's always hammers, isn't it?" He almost lost it. Yes. It was the end of the world. Voids knew that the situation was bad. But they were trying to make the best of a completely comet foxtrot situation, and they could really use a break from the galaxy. Right now.

Instead, there was a horrible tearing sound as a droid cut through the hallway, unable to get through the airlock that Abe had permanently damaged. Through the gouged-out holes, they could see what looked like brightly glowing red eyes, which were most likely the infrared scanners of the Hunter Killer droids. In the flicker lights and sparks thrown up by their cutters, they looked like nightmares.

CHAPTER 12

Bik's Gatling railgun roared to life, spitting out rounds upon thousands of rounds of depleted uranium at the opening. Immediately, the two Rahmani brothers kneeled in flanking positions on the big heavy weapons specialist, taking cover behind the recessed hallway segments and firing short, controlled bursts.

Ramirez and Kelly stood behind those firing, Kelly with one hand on Bik's shoulder, directing his fire occasionally, while Ramirez began assembling a metal apparatus. For a moment, Tai and Dax were a little bombasted, unable to act, but they shook themselves out of it and took positions standing behind the Rhamani brother's kneeling positions and unloaded. Not that the hunter killer droids seemed to be phased by all the ammunition being sent their way.

From the corner of his vision, he saw Ramirez click a few

more metal pieces in place and then held her hand over a button. The contraption glowed yellow and hummed. "Bik, platform! Abe, Far, cover him!"

Bik heaved the beast of gun, and then headed to Ramirez's position, while the two brothers, after tapping the two civilians on their legs, stood up and laid down a withering barrage of fire.

Within a few moments, Bik had set up his huge gun on the platform Ramirez and constructed. "Fall back!" Ramirez yelled, and the two brothers tactically retreated, taking a step back between each burst before ducking below the heavy weapon's field of fire and stepping behind him. Far paused momentarily to tap on a wall before ducking behind it. Dax and Tai followed their lead, scrambling for cover.

Ramirez depressed the button. "Engage!" A yellow field sprung from the sides and top of the platform. It rose to about chest height, and with practiced movements, the four other marines knelt on either sides of Bik and fired over the shield.

At this point, two hunter killers had successfully cut their way through the airlock and were beginning to spin up their guns. Ramirez dove for one of the bags and pulled out a violent-looking tube and tossed it at Far, who hefted it over his shoulder and took aim through the viewfinder. Meanwhile, Ramirez pulled a small missile and loaded it into the rear of the tube, tapped on Far's helmet, covered her ears, and leaned away.

"Missile out," Far said, and the rest of the squad ducked or leaned away from the back blast of the missile. It took the first Hunter Killer droid in the arm and it tottered for a few moments before its eyes dimmed and the entire frame slacked and then collapsed.

Bik resumed his barrage but yelled over his shoulder, "How many more of those do we have, Sergeant?"

"Not enough for what's back there trying to kill us," she said, holding three more missiles in her arms. In response, Abe turned and grabbed an object from his side pocket.

"Scrambler out!" and again the other squad mates ducked and leaned against the hull recesses as Abe tossed out a grenade that exploded in a fury of silver snow. It temporarily blinded and stunned the drones, who moved their heads aimlessly in a scanning, tracking motion.

"Smash and move," Ramirez said, loading one more missile in the launcher Far held, the last two strapped to her flak jacket. She tapped Far's helmet, and he shot off the missile and then stood up and collected his gear.

The rest of the squad set off a few more volleys of fire and stood up as well.

"Are you grabbing the force field?" Tai asked, hitching her gear on her shoulders.

"No, it has a proximity self-destruct," Far. "Should slow some of them down."

A few moments later, they heard it explode.

"Ammo and weapons check, people," Ramirez said when they got to the next hallway and had closed up the airlock behind them. The rest of the marines cycled their weapons and checked their charges. Bik looked at the mass count for his drum and then gave a thumbs-up. So did Kelly and Abe.

Far was inspecting the wall and shook his head. "No luck," he said to his brother.

Abe shook his head also. "We're low on mechanical interdiction, Sarge. I guess I figured that we wouldn't be facing a lot of mechanicals out there, with the Tactum down and all."

"It's not any of your fault. You prioritized where you thought you had to." Ramirez looked at her wristcom display which was tracking the drones. "Abe, got any signal magic for us yet?"

"Nothing. Like I said, their protocol is very strict. It's meant to track people who might have attempted to hack the IFF databases, just like we did." He was scrolling through his wristcom, which was laden with lines upon lines of code. "I mean, they really are just doing their job as best as they can."

"Unfortunately," Dax said, "Their job is to voiding kill us."

Everyone nodded gravely.

"We got a few more halls before we reach the cargo bay. Let's put a little hustle on this."

"Zeph," Tai said over her comms. "I hope this doesn't need mentioning, but you better be ready to haul some serious astrogator behind when we get there."

"Five by five on that, Tai. I've had the navcom crunching the numbers on our gate jump, and I have a few escape jumps in the system in case things get hairy." He paused. "Which they just did."

Far looked up from his wristcom when Zeph paused. "You reading what I am reading, astrogator?"

"'Fraid so."

"Voids."

"What is it, specialist?" Ramirez asked, voicing Dax's own concerns.

"Remember how I said the drones operate on a cascading threat analysis?"

"Yes, yes," Abe said, pulling up next to his brother, short of breath. "But honestly, we mostly phase you out when you talk artificial intelligence."

Far actually look hurt, turning from his brother to his Sergeant. Ramirez raised her hand and gave a "so-so" gesture.

"Well, it means, for one, that they can use misdirection and change up their tactics." He pulled up his wrist screen for everyone. "What do you see?"

"Nothing," Tai said, squinting.

"Exactly. They just changed up their tactics from chainsaw massacre to stealth ninja."

"Hunter Killer stealth ninjas," Zeph chimed in.

Several of their group swore, while Bik made the sign of the cross. It was followed by a large rumbling from behind the door they had just locked.

"We're Oscar Mike again, folks. Abe, crash and bang this hallway." The rest of the squad divvied up Abe's load, while he rigged up several IEDs. He set up a few conventional anti-personal and anti-drone devices before locking the airlock. He leaned on one of the side halls, catching his breath.

A giant spike pierced through the wall, impaling Abe through the ribs.

"Abe!" Far yelled, just as Ramirez yelled, "Contact right!"

Bik and Kelley opened fire above Abe's slumped figure. Abe was doubled over, hands over the gaping hole in his chest. Far and Ramirez dove for him, Bik and Kelley letting up their fire for the few seconds it took the other two to drag Abe to safety before opening up again. Dax felt useless firing off his sidearm but it was all he could do. It was Tai who had the field medic experience.

"How is he?" Far asked, cradling his brother's head.

"Not good," Tai said, pressing a compact dressing on the wound. "If we don't get him to the Kyrie's med bay in under an hour, he might go under or just die from blood loss and shock."

Ramirez punched the steel floor. "They flanked us. They used the explosions to cover up their true objective, and then took us from the side where we weren't expecting."

"I got an emergency route plotted for you all," Zeph said over the radio. "If you can get out of the hallway of death."

Dax was about to say something, when Far stopped, dropped the bags of supplies he was carrying, and turned to face not the droids but the wall.

He touched the surface and seemed to be satisfied with what he found. "Finally." With a few punches in his wrist comm, he activated a console on the side of the wall. Part of the hallway pulled away, and an equipment array bay slid out, holding an armed mechanized suit.

CHAPTER 13

Dax watched in amazement as Far calmly pulled a command console from the bay and brought the mech suit to life. “Kelly, Sergeant, if you could get my brother out of here, I’ll cover your retreat.”

Kelly looked from Far to Abe and then back to Far. “Cover our retreat, as in, you will be following right after, correct?”

“Of course, Kelly,” he lied.

Bik was laying down covering fire while Kelly and Ramirez held Abe between them. He came up to his brother’s figure and kissed his forehead. “Shallam, my brother,” he said, draping his shemagh over him. “You are as beautiful as our mother.”

“Shallam,” Abe said, weekly, barely able to open his eyes.

Bik and Ramirez alternated fire, covering Kelly as she

dragged Abe through the lock while Dax and Tai tossed the supplies through it. They were going through their meager supply of ammunition at an alarming rate but the scrubbers and the cells were still intact, and that meant that the Kyrie could fly.

Far, on the other hand, had almost entirely rigged the suit. It was an augmented defense platform, meant to repel invaders in close quarters combat. The left arm held a large ballistic shield and a wicked looking spiked pylon, the right a large bore grenade launcher. Chain guns flanked the suit's shoulders.

He started lobbing explosive after explosive into the writhing mass of drones, jamming the pylon into the face of any of them that got too close. When Kelly confirmed that Abe was secure on the other side, they formed an orderly retreat, with Far taking the point of the wedge, flanked by Bik and Kelly on one side, Ramirez and Tai on the other.

"Tell me when you are through," Far said, through gritted teeth, "and I'm going to rush forward to give you a little space."

Kelly and Tai came through, grabbing their bags and hauling them down the next hall. Then Bik, maneuvering his large gun through the opening, took one last look at friend, grabbed his gear, and turned to follow the other two. Just because Far was holding their rear didn't mean that some drones might not be trying to cut them off from the dock.

Ramirez stepped through next, firing off a few more shots from her rifle before grabbing another bag of gear. She stopped. "Specialist Farrhid Rahmani, it was an honor to serve with you."

"And with you."

She saluted him, and he returned with a nod, right arm attached to the controls of the grenade launcher and the chain guns that were temporarily silent.

Dax felt a tap at his leg, and he looked down to see Abe lifting his hand, asking to be pulled up. He hoisted the marine up, bag over the other shoulder. He was pale and bloodstained, but he looked determined. He gulped a few times, working his mouth. He turned to his brother.

"Allahu Akbar!" he yelled, at the top of his lung, the considerable strain showing in the veins of his neck, and the twinge of pain racking his side.

Without turning, Far yelled back. "Allahu Akbar!" God is greater.

And for a few glorious moments, Far fought like his God was greater than the combined might of technology arrayed against him, an avenging angel against a host of demon nightmares.

CHAPTER 14

When Dax shut the second airlock door behind him, putting a whole hallway between him and the drones, he was greeted with solemn looks. Kelly was almost outright sobbing, her tiny frame shaking with every breath. Even Tai, who put forward a calm facade had sadness tinging her eyes.

Ramirez pulled up her wristcom. "Astrogator, do you read our path as clear?"

"I voiding hope so, Miss Sergeant sir," Zeph said, butchering both the title and rank in one go. "I still suggest haste. I'm not liking the sympathetic vibrations I'm reading in the station's structure."

"You heard the man," Ramirez said. "Let's move out, squad." She looked at Tai and him. "And civilians."

"Useful civilians," Dax said.

"Very useful." She was grim faced and determined. She had probably lost many comrades and marines today, but this last one seemed to be taking its toll.

They reached the final airlock and Dax looked over this motley crew of survivors. The practical side of him put them on scales. Did the additional skills outweigh the additional resources they would drain on their ship?

"Zeph," he said through his wristcom, "we're coming out. Party of six."

"Six? I thought there were seven of you." Zeph spoke, distracted, probably pumping in some mass recalculations to see if there were more aggressive inertia saving maneuvers the Kyrie could pull off with one less passenger.

"Just prepare for six."

"Right on, boss." Zeph said. "Just as long as you got supplies for the Kyrie. She's mighty hungry."

Dax stepped out into the empty void of space, and there, sitting amidst the destruction and desolation, was a humble light transport ship, mostly nondescript, very banged up…but in Dax's eyes, she was the most beautiful lady in the system.

"I've got eyes on Kyrie." Dax started the slow yet insistent pace of latching and releasing mag boots. The marines, almost on instinct, took positions behind him, putting him in the lead. Dax knew, from his Cooperative Navy days, that marines knew to take the lead in surface based operations but naturally paid the proper amount of subservience when on a ship or craft. Fingers crossed, there would not be too much trouble concerning matters of command. Zeph opened the cargo bay doors and Tai and Dax took positions on either side of the bay, stowing the supplies that the marines handed to them.

"Med Bay?" Bik said after laying his gun on the ground.

Tai nodded and accompanied the big guy to Kyrie's med bay.

The cargo bay doors closed and the mag lifts released, and for a moment he got the special kind of vertigo that accompanied rapid changes in gravity…which left once Zeph spun up the artgrav generators. Dax made his way to the cockpit, and with haste, got buckled into his chair.

"Not a moment too soon, Cap. I'm getting radiological warnings from the Boh."

"You mean?"

"Yup," Zeph sad, tapping one of his display monitors, making a copy of it with a split finger motion and sliding the copy over to Dax's console. "Orbital standoff yield, based off the readings."

He couldn't find an appropriate curse. It felt, that since the world had ended, every hand they had been dealt had been hammers. It reminded him of that bad streak on… he couldn't remember the backwater solar systems name anymore—but he had actually woken up naked in an alley.

"Are we clear Zeph?"

"Mag locks released, I assume you are going hands-on?"

"Well there aren't really any nav satellites out there to autopilot for us, so I was leaning towards yes."

"I've plotted an approach vector to the Ring. I've passed the path to your console." Zeph flicked a few fingers and Dax saw the vector as a blue curve on his screen. "Please note the relative velocities to avoid, you know, destruction from temporal spatial forces exerted during Ring travel."

"Yikes, almost forgot about that. That means I can't just hightail it to the Ring." Dax bit his lip as he reviewed the vector. "Tai, I'm going to need you here on the weapons console," he said over ship speakers

"I'm almost there," came the response from Tai's wristcom.

"How are our special guests? Situated?"

"I gave them the impending apocalypse essentials tour. Our friend in med bay seems to be stabilized as well, which is all moot if the Bohoja starts firing at us."

"We are all strapped in, Captain," Ramirez said from her own wristcom.

"Good, good. Uh, imagine I gave some very inspiring speech there, and I'm ending it with 'and brace for possible impact.'"

"I feel appropriately inspired."

At that moment, Tai came barreling through the airlock and threw herself into her chair, firing up to orange brilliance her myriad of weapon HUDs and readouts.

Dax switched from onboard comms to wrist comms. When the ship started firing munitions and going hard burn for evasive maneuvers, they would not be able to hear each otherwise. “I’m going hands-on. Zeph, make yourself useful and help out Tai.”

“Right on Cap. I should mention that I have spin up readings for the automated defenses for both the Bohoja and Mamoru. The Mamoru’s probably in response to the Boh’s radiological readings, and the Boh’s in response to Mamoru’s spinning up her automated defenses.”

Tai handed Zeph a few HUDs to manage. While Zeph was a genius in multitasking information consoles, Tai was a poet when it came to weapon heads up displays.

“Perfect. Perfect.” Dax grunted as the ship started responding to his controls, trying to delicately use the retro thrusters to get out of the dilapidated bay. “Heads up, boys and girls, the moment we clear this bay, we’re going to start firing.”

He rotated the ships orientation to line up with Zeph’s approach vector. The empty black of a universe that no longer cared about them spun into the brilliant lights of multicolored streaks and explosions of a solar system that wanted to destroy them.

CHAPTER 15

Once, Dax had been punched in the head, really hard. Dax had been punched many times in his career as an on-and-off again illegal transporter of questionable goods. But what had made this punch memorable was how it was not.

The events following and preceding that punch had been lost in the concussive haze of the interaction. Tai had pulled him out of some mess he had started with his big mouth again—he had confirmed later. There was illicit PFCs, a card game (there was always a card game), a pretty girl (there were never was enough pretty girls), and a lot of angry words, according to Tai. But to him, when he tried to remember that span of time, the only thing he could recollect was the explosion of colors when a thug had brought a charged knuckle duster to his left temple.

The scene before him gave off a nauseating episode of déjà vu.

"Are you hands-on?" Tai's voice came as an incessant, if not overly panicked buzz in his headset.

"You bet your chips I am," he said with a grunt, maneuvering the Kyrie into a stomach dropping dive to keep a building-size piece of debris between his starboard and the Bohoja. Which was destroyed by the impact of anti-spacecraft flack only moments later.

"I hate it when you say 'bet,' it brings back a lot of bad memories."

He wanted to nod in response, but, again, the nausea. So he just grunted more.

"We're deviating a bit from the approach vector, Cap'n," Zeph reminded him.

"You just keep posting more theoretical firing solutions and I'll worry about the damn vector." More explosions. The Ring was on his port side. A tight corkscrew maneuver made it on his starboard again.

"You do know that if we approach the Ring even a single azimuth off, the Eigen forces involved will—"

Dax turned to give Zeph a glare, which did nothing to improve his stomach's constitution. "You are going to lecture me about an uncertain death when a highly probable one is in front of us in the shape of TWO giant orbital standoff stations and the metric tons of ammunition and ordinance they have between them?"

Zeph paused. "Cap'n," he started, almost timidly, "you do know that just because the forces exist in a 'quantum uncertainty field,' doesn't mean we aren't sure they happen, right? I mean, it's been tested. The Quantum Uncertainty field means that . . ."

"Yes, yes Observer, something something. I passed navigation physics." He hadn't. His instructors in flight school at basic training had said they had rarely seen anyone so incompetent in basic navigational physics that passed. But, he was a natural talent at the stick.

A talent that he was pushing to its limit now.

Sirens began wailing on Zeph's console. "I've got five missiles locked on and toned to the Kyrie."

"Give me their paths."

Five different trajectories appeared on his console. "What is this garbage hand you are trying to deal me, Zeph?"

"Three are from different Bohoja defense sats, one is from the Boh himself and the last one . . ."

"Don't you say it,"

". . . is from the Mamoru."

"I hate this solar system!" Dax pulled the Kyrie into a more forceful barrel roll than necessary, but spinning in the opposite direction seemed to calm down his stomach. A little.

"Uh, is everything okay up there?" Ramirez's voice came over the comms. "I mean, okay in reference to the end of the world."

"No," Dax said, trying to keep the edge off his voice. "Everything is not okay." Explosions off the port side. Another barrel roll. Nope. Now they were making his stomach worse. "I need you and your marines on the point defense guns, Romeo Foxtrot November."

"Wait," Ramirez said, after a pause, "this transport class vessel has point defenses?"

"Space pirates sergeant. Space pirates! Just," he shook his head to clear his vision. "Just, please. Lecture later."

Ramirez gave the professional double click on her comm in accent.

"Zeph, can you share those trajectories to everyone?" Tai asked.

"With what? The Tactum is down, how can—" Tai pointed at Zeph's forehead and then her headset. "Oh yeah, jumping on the marine short band frequency now."

And even now, as Zeph pumped more and more vector data into the lone, overtaxed, non-networked algebraic logic unit, and the marines and Tai took up Kyrie's point defense weaponry, Dax was alone.

All of this was happening in Dax's periphery, of course, but it did not involve him, per se. No, his world was a tight dance among the stars involving a very neat and idealized approach vector and a host of hot and messy firing solutions. Among the brilliant sea of explosions, pattern recognition, and improvisation were his only companions. He saw the Kyrie's point defenses take out the five anti-aircraft seeking missiles but those missiles might have been pointed at another ship, in another solar system, as far as it affected him.

He was threading a needle of pure light among the warp and weave of destruction.

And then from the frequency shadows of the firing solutions, a sixth missile appeared.

CHAPTER 16

Dax jerked. Hard.

Hard enough to give Zeph whiplash as he tried to sputter out the phrase "evasive maneuvers."

More alarms, but this time throughout the ship, accompanied by flashing red threat lights.

This one was persistent, staying firmly on his tail. Dax pulled another maneuver, skirting even closer than was prudent to the edge of an active firing solution and then releasing the last of his countermeasures. It stung, a little, to think how expensive each of those charged decoys were. But then, human life, his in particular, was also at a premium. That eased the pain. It made it sting less, anyway.

The missile shrugged off the trail of flairs.

"Cap," Tai said, "I'm sure you know these lights aren't just to look pretty."

"I'm trying, but this bastard is very persistent. I can't . . ."

His arm spasmed, causing his elbow to bang on the edge of the console. It was taking its toll, trying to keep the firing solutions and the approach vector visualized, as well as trying to throw evasive maneuvers into the mix.

"I can't, I can't . . ."

"Cap, you five by five there?" Tai asked.

"I can't shake it, Tai."

"Hey, leave it to us. You ain't the only one fighting for our lives here, okay?"

"Dax," Tai said, as if using his first name would anchor him. "Hold this course, until the missile stabilizes its bearing and hard locks. And then on my mark, at impact minus two seconds, pop a corkscrew, okay?"

She didn't even wait for him to nod before she started plotting out the shot solution on her console. Dax flew. Tai shot. That was the arrangement.

It was like flying air patrol on the Epsilon belt conflict all over again. He took a deep breath to steady his nerves and gripped the controls tight.

"Tango is stabilizing, Tai."

"Hold her steady."

And then, it was gone. The shaking. The sweat. The second guessing. He was frosty, he was glass, he was precision incarnate.

"Mark."

With controlled and effortless hand movements, Dax put the Kyrie in a lateral spin at the same time he dipped her nose and put her thrusters over cockpit, juking the missile and presenting her underbelly.

And her largest gun.

Tai fired off a pre-plotted solution, a starburst pattern that surrounded the missile in timed concussive blasts that formed a solid flak wall and then a lone piercing blast that did not concuss but instead punched straight into the ordnance.

The missile "bounced," temporarily blind and deaf of Kyrie's signature, a child blindfolded and then spun around for a birthday game. It pinged wildly, setting off a multitude of acquisition alarms in the ship, found tone, reoriented—

And was blasted apart by a five-thousand-millimeter flak shell from Mamoru's firing solution.

For one glorious moment, there were no threat alarms, no tone alarms, no radiological alarms to be heard in the cockpit. Dax savored that moment.

After a pause, Dax thumbed his comms. "Tai."

"Yes Cap."

"You know how I always give you a grief for spending all that time in combat simulators?"

"Yes Cap."

"Well, I sure am glad you ignore me when you feel like."

"Yes Cap. Pleasure to do so again in the future, Cap."

"Approach vector confirmed to within point five percent

accepted deviation. Make for two twenty-five by seventy-six." Zeph read off his console in an almost machine-like trance. "Coming about now. Correction. Correction. Hold." Zeph had to continuously check the navcom to ensure that Dax entered the Ring at a vector that was parallel to the foci of the Ring. "Approach vector confirmed to three percent accepted deviation."

The trick was to get it as close to absolute without crossing it in the process. Because you risked touching Eigenvector zero, zero, zero, zero. The void.

"Within point oh oh eight accepted deviation." This time he looked up, and returned to his human voice. "That should be a deviation of the no uncertain death kind, Captain."

Dax gave Zeph an appreciative nod. "Sounds good, Astrogator," he said, finding himself returning to his Cooperative Marine formalities. "Five by five, holding course."

He allowed himself a small measure of decompression, exhaling gratefully a breath that seemed like he had held for ages. A breath that had been caught in the pit of his stomach since they had left Mamoru.

He flipped the switch for onboard comms. "This is your Captain speaking. We will soon be leaving Pica, via the local Ring in the system. For all of you who are members of our Frequent Apocalypse Miles program, you will be earning three point five million light years on today's Ring jump." He paused, bringing up the scene behind them on the onscreen display in the cockpit "Please put your trays and seat backs in the upright and secure positions and stow all loose items for zero gravity transition as we begin jump checks and calculations to leave this murder system."

On the screen monitor, he had muted the radiological alarms that were now in hell scream pitch. A deceptively slow barrage of lights were expelled from the bellies of the Boh and the Mamoru.

"And thank you," he finished, "for flying post-Apocalyptic air."

"Approach vector confirmed." Zeph said. "Eigenvalues have harmonized and transcending to higher order dimensions. The Kyrie is now entering the Ring's quantum uncertainty field well."

"Punch it."

Behind them, the two Orbital Stand-Off Weapons mutually assured each other's destruction in the purifying light of thermo nuclear ordnance, ensuring that this system would be, for the foreseeable and relativistic future, an uninhabitable wasteland.

But to the ship's crew, they were simply bright albedo bodies crying streaks of fierce brightness against a dark background of the void.

And so, when the last lights fell from the sky, Dax knew that the end of this solar system, if not the entire galaxy, had truly begun.

PART TWO
GAMMA

CHAPTER 17

By all accounts, the Rings predated humanity by, well, a lot. History wasn't Dax's forte.

But they had been there, floating, in the emptiness of space, until twenty-third century explorers had chanced upon then, near the outskirts of Alpha Centauri. The colossal structures must have been awe inspiring and daunting back then. Hammers, they were still awe inspiring now, centuries later.

And they had completely changed the face of space travel, from the Alpha onward. To be able to reach to the stars without having to say goodbye to the entire world you were leaving behind was a gift upon all humankind that had to be shared, whether by Our Cooperative or The People's Republic.

Though it was just as good for escaping a self-destructing

solar system.

"Punch it." Dax said.

Zeph complied, pumping in the finalized approach vector.

When the Kyrie was close enough to be detected by the Ring, it powered itself on. No detectable source powered the Ring. Maybe was powered the ley lines of the galaxy itself.

"Never gets old, Cap" Tai said, feeling secure enough to look up from her tactical console, and took the sight in, just as entranced as the first time Dax had seen her watch it.

And the sight was just as mesmerizing for him. Colored a haunting, luminescent blue, the rift field gave the impression of a deep, cold ocean whose depths sunk below even the grasp of understanding. Kyrie crossed this threshold, plunging itself into Ring.

By all applicable and intelligible science available to them, upon crossing the rift field, they were destroyed. Picked apart atom by atom, and then transferred into, something. Something unknowable, impossible, and glorious. And that thing crossed the galaxy and thrust them into . . .

Emptiness.

"Status?" Dax asked.

Zeph looked at Dax quizzically. "Captain, no Tactum remember? No positional telemetry, no live feed. What do you expect? I refresh the Navcom," Zeph entered a keystroke, "and all I'm gonna get is a whole lot of nothing . . ." The onscreen display showed an astrogation map. It wasn't live, as was evident by the "Loss of Signal" and "Offline" warnings in the corner of the screen, but these were not locally stored map data.

Zeph shook his head. "Ohwowhat in the galaxy . . ." he went through a few more keystrokes.

"So, status?"

"Well, the maps that shouldn't be generating from a communication method that doesn't exist claim we are in the Gamma system. And from basic star positioning it's the right cluster, in the very least."

"You're saying," Tai said, "that somehow our astrogation data was updated?"

"Not just updated. T-updated. As in, by Tactum, which—"

"Doesn't exist." Tai finished.

There was silence in thought. "It's not back, is it?" Dax asked. "Or was it only system wide?"

Zeph checked on his console. 'No active T-signals in this locality. I'm not able to ping a single sat in the system."

The comm system to the bridge chirped. "Captain, this Sergeant Ramirez, asking permission to enter the bridge."

"This ain't an Our Cooperative Ship, Theresa. If you ain't trying to kill or harm me, Tai, or Zeph, you got permission to be on the bridge." In fact, they had enough space and consoles to seat all of them on the bridge. It would be a tight fit, but it would be nice to have the Kyrie fully manned.

There was a momentary pause as the bridge unsealed, revealing a disheveled and perturbed Theresa Ramirez, Sergeant. She held up a data. "I just got a system specific sitrep, Our Cooperative official."

"Well that's good, right?" Tai said. "Those always have up-to-date telemetry for all nearby planets and systems, and military risk assessments for all major forces and governments in the local."

"Yes, very useful, but you see, I didn't expect to ever see an official OCMC sitrep because these were transmitted via Tactum, which—"

"Doesn't exist," All three of them said emphatically to Ramirez, and then broke into small fits of laughter. Grim laughter kept the Kyrie afloat.

She coughed, a little surprised by the outburst. "This is not a laughing matter, Captain."

"Trust me, Sergeant. At this point, everything is a laughing matter," Dax wiped a tear from his eye. "But, yes, we experienced something similar with our astrogation data feeds." He turned to Zeph. "What time stamp do you have on those maps?"

"From zero four thirteen, ship time."

"And yours, Theresa?"

The Sergeant looked at the data pad. "Oh, let me sync to ship time." She pressed a few buttons on the screen. "Zero four thirteen as well."

“Well, that places it around the time we jumped so,” Dax said, scratching the scruff that was starting to grow on his face. It had been, what, a day and a half ship time since he had last shaved. “What other possible sources other than the Tactum?”

“Well, it couldn’t have come from Pica,” Tai said. “Or any other system for that matter. It would take, what, centuries for us to receive that signal through electromagnetic frequencies?”

“Try centuries upon centuries,” Zeph said. “Not accounting for deterioration. The energy it would have taken to transmit this much data over that much space?” Zeph made a poofing magic gesture with his fingers.

This is why the Tactum had so nefariously pervaded every aspect of their lives. It was just too damn convenient. Unlimited bandwidth, instantaneous transmission.

“And it could not have come here, in Gamma or wherever we are,” Ramirez said, flipping her data pad around so they could see it. “No active signals in this locality.”

“So that leaves one place it could have happened, right?” Dax said. “It had to have happened in the Ring.”

“The Ring,” Zeph said, in a whisper.

It was now the only life link between these solar systems, set afloat in this black sea of empty. Dax couldn’t even imagine how lonely and far away the galaxy, let alone the entire universe, must have felt when humankind had first set out with only liquid-based rockets and electromagnetic communication.

Dax lowered their blast shields to reveal the bridge's portholes. He touched the cold duraglass and looked through it into the emptiness. Early astrogators had called the vast stretches of nothing between known space as "the Void." Emptiness that stretched farther than could be traveled in one lifetime. The Void separated humanity just as effectively as any wall could. More effectively.

"Zeph, any tachyon particle emissions from the Ring?"

"As far as I can read, and let's be honest the Ring has stumped equipment a lot more sophisticated than ours, but as far as I can read, nothing."

No one was coming through that Ring. No help. No support. No survivors.

"Your Ma and Pa were on Pica 6, weren't they, Zeph."

Zeph was quiet for a moment. Then there was a sharp intake of breath before he spoke. "My whole family. Mema and Pawpa, my little sisters. My dog." Another sharp intake of breath. "Voids, my dog."

"You Ramirez?"

"My entire operational formation was on the 'moru." She flipped her data pad, and a burst of gold ID tags appeared in the space in front of her. "We lost a lot of comrades and friends today." On the bottom of the display a message of "Chain of Command not found" blinked.

He didn't need to ask Tai. He knew where her family was.

Dax didn't have much family, and he preferred it that way. When they had dropped of their cargo on Pica 5, they had been given one blissful night of reprieve planetside. There had been a pretty purple-eyed, black-haired girl he had danced with all night. A rare night not spent at the card table. A rare night trying to make a genuine human connection. But when he had awoken the next morning, she had already left for her route, just transports ships crossing in the system.

He had already forgotten her name. He was probably starting to forget her face.

She was probably dead, along with the crew of the Luxuria they couldn't save and that unnamed ship that had tried. Along with the entire population of the Mamoru. And the Bohoja for that matter. And anyone within radiological distance of the Amaterasu, dying a fiery nuclear death, as the smaller sun imploded on itself. Actually, his napkin physics told him that a solar system wouldn't long outlive the loss of one of their suns . . .

He felt hands restraining him, and Ramirez and Tai were pulling him away from the porthole. There were red streaks on the thick glass, and his knuckles stung. His throat was raw. Had he been yelling? He could view the ring through the portal, the massive structure framing the void beyond it. Had he been screaming at the Void? Screaming at the Ring?

The Rings had bridged that void physically, but it had

been the Tactum that had bridged it intellectually, and for every voice in the galaxy, from one end to the other.

That distance felt vast now. And the Kyrie and her crew, a small voice screaming against the void.

CHAPTER 18

They sat in silence for quite some time. When Bik and Kelly reached they bridge, they caught on to the somber mood, arraying themselves on the extra seats without a word.

"So, what does it say?" Dax asked. The silence had become palpable.

"What does what say?" Ramirez asked.

"The OCMC sitrep? What does the Cooperative Marine Corp think of this system?" There was a good chance they were stuck here, after all.

She flicked through the report. "It's inquisitive," she said.

"The Corp can be inquisitive? In all my time with the Corp, it has been many things." Dax said. "Inquisitive has never been one of those things." He cracked a smile. Tried to.

"Well some of us do ask questions when we aren't too

busy eating crayons." She slipped comfortably into the friendly banter between pilot and ground pounder. "Not inquisitive in general, but in very specific things." Ramirez placed her pad in holo mod again, the gold ID's replaced by a projected diagram. "One of the planets in this system has a high powered planetside satellite array, and science division thought that since this system was at a Ring junction the satellite could be put to use monitoring possible emissions."

Zeph turned in his chair, facing the Marine Sergeant. "But Rings don't generate any emissions, electromag or otherwise. All the energy comes from traversal through it."

"You don't know the military, Zeph," Tai said, a grin on her face. "When brass says 'jump,' the only question you ask is—"

"How high," Dax said.

Ramirez chimed in, "And when the brass says, 'investigate and find evidence of an impossible phenomena with a planetside satellite,' the only question you ask is,"

"Which planet," Dax finished.

Zeph was quiet for a moment as the Sergeant and the retired military personnel chuckled between themselves.

"Gamma Four, right?" Zeph said, breaking their revelry.

"What," Ramirez said, arching an eyebrow.

"The planet, with the satellite. It's Gamma Four, right?"

"Yes. How did you know?" Ramirez said, bringing up the system diagram that highlighted the fourth planet from the single sun in the system.

"Well, I might not be military, retired or otherwise, but I can recognize a high-powered planetside satellite broadcasting in the clear as easily as the next fellow. Well, given that that fellow has basic comms training," Zeph said, tapping the side of his head, almost smug. Then Zeph gave the Sergeant a big wink. Dax mentally scratched the "almost."

Ramirez scrunched her forehead together on that last part. Dax was starting to realize that it meant something was worrying her. She had worn it a lot in the past hours.

"In the clear, you said?" Ramirez waited for Zeph to nod. "Well, what are you waiting for?"

Zeph tilted his head, not sure what she was getting at.

"Play the damn thing!"

"Oh, yes, yes, of course." Because it had been broadcast in the clear, it meant it was not encrypted. And if it was not encrypted, then that meant someone had a message so important that they would risk anyone, even a potential enemy, hearing it.

Within the time it took Zeph to receive and decompress the message—single point array did not have the bandwidth of the Tactum—the rest of Ramirez's squad, excluding Abe who was still in the med bay, had arranged themselves and their consoles into the now cozy bridge.

It was a tight fit but Dax realized, looking around, that in the end of the world, he preferred the coziness to the stark emptiness that usually accompanied them on their travels.

Zeph fed the broadcast from his console into the ship comms, a sound wave graph projecting on the main display. He dimmed the bridge lights. "Presentation matters, you know?" With a dramatic flair, he pressed a button on his console. A tight buzz came over the speakers.

And nothing else.

"Well, that's kinda…underwhelming," Kelly said.

"No, it's amazing. That's not regular static. It's generated white noise." Zeph seemed to bounce on his toes, oddly enough.

"Astrogator, maybe there is something I am missing here," Ramirez said, including her squad with her gesture, "but I don't see how generated white noise is any different from regular static."

"Well, for two reasons." Zeph stood up. "First, static is often generated when there is a transmission discrepancy. Misalignment of frequency modulation, insufficient hardware specs, or just general signal interference. But the fact that it is artificial generated means that none of this is an issue. Someone is purposefully adding the white noise."

"To what purpose?" Tai asked.

"Obviously to hide something." Zeph smiled. Expectantly.

"All right all right. I'll bite," Dax said. "Hiding what?"

Zeph's smile got bigger. "Well, the second reason generated white noise is different from regular transmission interference is that it is algorithmically generated. So, all one has to do is apply the reverse of that algorithm and . . ." Zeph pressed a button on his console, and then made a 'tada' gesture.

On-screen a second sound wave appeared. It joined with the first, and they cancelled each other out, leaving behind a smaller, tighter sound wave.

What seemed to be a random series of chirps and whistles emitted from the ship speakers.

"I second my 'underwhelming' comment from earlier, and add 'annoying,'" Kelly said, raising her hand.

Tai looked Zeph in the eye. "So?"

"So what?" Zeph asked.

"So what does it mean?"

Zeph's face showed momentary confusion. "How am I supposed to know? I'm just telling that someone is trying to hide this message underneath that generated white noise."

"Well, that is significant information," Ramirez said. "It speaks to intent. But," she gestured to the main display, "it would be magnitudes more helpful to know what the suppressed message said." She rubbed her forehead.

"Well I can't help you with the 'what,'" Zeph said. "But maybe I can help you with the 'where?'"

"I thought you said it was coming from Gamma 4?" Dax said.

"Yes, but not generated from the same source." Zeph

split the sound wave into signal components and static components. "The statics is being generated from the comm station mentioned in the Sergeant's sitrep. But instead of directing high energy emissions into the direction of the Ring's event horizon, it has been jerry rigged into a hi-fi emitter."

"That's possible?" Tai asked.

"Well, if the necessary equipment is on hand. And if you have the know-how." Zeph counted off the reasons on his hand. "Oh, and if you are willing to lose a lot of transmission power."

"And the other source?"

"It's a step-up transmitter. Very local focused. And what's interesting is, based off of the wave form, this signal is very powerful within close proximity."

"Isn't that true for all radio signals?" Tai said. She brought up her tac console. "Our tight beam emitter loses a lot of fidelity the further out it goes."

"That is generally true, but radio waves can be modulated to prefer amplitude over wavelength, or rather power versus distance. The decay pattern on the hidden wave indicates it is very powerful in the locality." He pulled the wave pattern and set it against a distance axis.

"Within a light second or so, the pattern is actually stronger than the comm station's satellite array. Stepped down transmission power, right?" He pulled the graph further out to the left. "Outside of that range, however, the satellite array starts overcoming the local emitter. You can see in the eleven ExaHertz—"

"So what does that tell us?" Ramirez interjected. "Not to be rude, astrogator, or disparage your very impressive presentation."

"Thanks for that," Zeph said, and Ramirez returned him a wink and a thumbs-up.

"But either way, what does it tell us? We have ventured out of the academic question of the end of the world, to a practical one."

"It tells us," Tai said, "that someone is very set on making sure that signal does not leave the planet," referring to the local emitter's wave graph. "Enough so that they would paralyze a military research grade sat array."

"But why?" Kelly said. She threw up her hands, speaking with force. "It's just a series of beeps and whistles. What do they even mean? What are they?"

"They're drone commands," a weak voice said over the intercom, and punctuated the statement with a cough.

CHAPTER 19

Ramirez brought her wristcom up. "Private, I am pretty sure that you still should be resting after that round of cellular regrowth."

There was no response. Ramirez depressed the blister on her wristcom again.

"Private, respond?"

The bridge air lock opened, revealing a pale faced and disheveled Abe.

Kelly gasped. "Abe, what are you doing?" She rushed over, but Abe forestalled her.

"Sorry, sorry, you were pumping all of that audio through the ship speaker, and well . . ." Abe shrugged, but he did have the good sense to blush. "Anyway, no vital organs." He lifted his shirt, and his skin had the graph paper-like texture of a rapidly regrown skin cells. Fresh of the Creche, they would say.

"Far is the drone specialist, but." Abe paused with a cough. "I mean, Far was the drone specialist, but he made sure I learned a lot about drone basics. He was annoying like that." Dax could feel the emotion tinging the word "annoying."

"Either way, that's basic DCTP, Drone Control-Tactum Protocol. But in analogue form." He shook his head. "And, obviously, being broadcasted over electromagnetic frequencies, not T-freqs."

"That's, that'sthewhatwhy." It was Zeph's turn to throw up his hands. That's barbaric. You'd suffer so much latency and signal decay. It's like, what's that thing," Zeph snapped his fingers as he looked for the word. "Wifi! That thing, you know."

He was met with blank stares.

"It's the wireless data communication from a few centuries ago." He smacked his head. "Voids, do none of you holo anything other than entertainment serials?"

"OCN arms reports," Tai said.

"Galaxy Poker Championship series," Dax said.

"I-dramas," Bik said. Everyone turned to him. "I admit, I am entranced by the central system dramas. The Imperial intrigue and machinations. It is a guilty pleasure of mine."

"Okay: obvious, addict, and pleasantly surprising, but no judgement," Zeph said, pointing to each of them in turn. "But seriously, holo some history every so often." He mumbled something that sounded like 'rot your brains.'

"Either way," Abe said, limping over to a free inertia seat and console, and dumping himself roughly into it. "Wooh, sorry, standing is hard. But either way, someone is trying to use that emitter to take control of T-drones."

"But they would need some sort of ad-hoc transmitter acting as a drone controller, and to do that—"

"Okay, but first," Dax said, turning to Zeph to interrupt him, "I can stop anytime I want, and second, what kind of drones are out there?"

Ramirez pulled up her sitrep. "The system census says Gamma 4 is mostly an agricultural planet."

"Agri-drones. Hardly a threat," Dax said.

"My home planet is part of an agri-drone network," Bik said. "The tribe nations get a huge kickback to lease their lands for agriculture production. I would not want to face a thresher drone alone, or even with a full weapon squad."

Dax reconsidered. "Okay, so someone on that planet might have an army of farm drones. Dangerous farm drones. But we know that someone is there. And I don't want to rain on how well the end of the world has been going for us so far, but while we were able to gather some supplies on the Mamoru, escaping her took a lot of them."

Ramirez sighed. "The Captain is right. Census says Gamma 4 should have a Marine Expeditionary Force FOB.

And a forward operating base means a fuel depot for small craft, at least."

"So it's decided then," Dax said. "We check out the planet with the possible army of murder bots. And if we're lucky—"

"Don't say 'lucky,'" Ramirez said.

"Don't say 'murder bot,'" Tai said.

"If we're lucky, we'll be in and out of the FOB without a hitch," Dax finished.

"You've doomed us all," Kelly said.

"Smells like a trap," Abe said, chewing a military food bar.

"Abe, you say everything smells like a trap," Bik said.

"And when I'm wrong, nobody dies."

"Traps or no traps. Unfortunately it's going to come down to logistics," Ramirez said. Fuel, air, water," she walked over to Abe and grabbed the food bar out of his hand. "Food." She took a bite.

"Hey, I've been saving that for a special occasion!"

"What special occasion?" Kelly asked.

"I'm alive ain't I, yaar?"

Ramirez looked each of them in the eye. Abe held his hand out, and Ramirez sighed. Abe wouldn't be mollified until she returned the bar. He happily went back to snacking. He would need to consume a lot of calories in the next few days to assist with the regrowth.

"We are still Our Cooperative Marines on a," She paused, and turned to Dax, question in her glance.

He nodded slightly. Then shrugged and nodded more forcefully.

"Cooperative Marines on a Cooperative vessel. Which means, ultimately, it is our captain who decides."

She was right. Technically.

Dax considered for a moment. "We could roll the dice again, jump into the Ring again without a live updated astrogation map, hope we come out in one piece. But it makes no sense with a most likely fully-stocked depot in this system. Even with the possibility of aggressive farming drones."

Tai leaned back against her console and nodded, and the rest of the marines did as well.

"Well we have to make sure that when we get dirtside that we try not to get distracted." He looked at Zeph for the last one.

Zeph just shrugged and looked at Tai questioningly.

Tai looked at purposefully Dax.

"Okay, I will try not to get distracted," Dax admitted.

"One more wrinkled in there Captain," Ramirez said, stiffening as she read something on her data pad.

"We got a beat-up ship that needs about every spare part left in the verse and that ain't wrinkle enough for y'all?"

"I found something in the transmission

"The Drone protocol?" Abe said. "I didn't catch it."

"No, in the generated white noise."

"Wait what?" Zeph pulled up the original wave form again. "Where. Who. How?"

"I invoked a standard OCMC decryption analysis on it."

"Aren't those different from system to system?" Tai asked

"Yes, but it responded to my rank and specialty." She tapped the Sergeants' Chevrons, then the Infantry designation beneath it.

"It's not too complex, but only Our Cooperative Forces, or retired, usually catch it." She pressed a few buttons on her data pad. "And just like so," she pressed a final button, the wave form transformed once more. They were no longer waves, but rather long and short dashes of high and low frequency.

"What is it?" Kelly asked.

"It's not a sound wave, I can tell you that," Zeph said, standing up to get a better look at the display. "Ah, the decryption converted the signal stream from analogue to digital. Maybe it's binary? The Highs are 1's and the lows are 0's?"

"Not binary, look," Abe said. "If you think of the highs as on keys, the lows as off keys, it's Morse code."

"Wow, that's going really far back. Prehistoric," Zeph said.

"Still a classical favorite for signal operators," Abe said. "But you are right, the T bandwidth makes it pretty inefficient." He looked at the sequence. "Do you mind if I use this console, Cap?"

Dax nodded. "Be my guest. Y'all make yourself feel at home."

Abe was at his console, despite the injury. "I'm going to take that form and convert it into Morse representation," he said as he worked. "Assuming that a single high is a dot, and three highs are a dash . . ." he spread his hands in triumph. "There we go!" On screen the tiered wave form converted into Morse code dashes and dots, complete with word spaces and end markations. Abe took a small bow.

Ramirez went up the screen inspected it, and looked at the signal specialist. "Abe, you idiot, none of us except you read Morse."

"Oh, sorry about that." Abe pressed another sequence of buttons on the console, and it translated into Cooperative Standard.

The entire bridge reeled, quiet and stunned.

"I told you," Abe said, breaking the silence, "bloody told you it was a bloody trap!"

CHAPTER 20

Dax let out a sigh that was as long and as deep as the galaxy. "Hammers." Another sigh, just for good measure to make sure the galaxy heard him. "It's always hammers."

"What does that even—" Kelly started.

But Tai cut her short. "Shh. Best not to interrupt when he starts waxing philosophical with poker terms."

"Will it offend him?" Kelly asked.

"No, worse. He'll try to explain it to you."

Dax ignored them. They had reviewed the message several times now, and Ramirez said it contained all the necessary protocol limiters."

"Mayday, mayday, OCMCMEF, calling all OCF. High priority package extraction requested. Opposition force present and hostile." It was appended with a sergeant Volkov ID tag and serial, which matched the in-system disposition, listing one Dimitri Ivanovich Volkov, OCMC.

"What do we know about the MEF elements here in this solar system? How did they fair when the Tactum collapsed?"

Ramirez pulled her data pad out again, and swiped from her pad to the main display, sending the entire feed over.

"The MEF did have a full company of Army engineers and Spacer research science fancy pants division" she highlighted a non-combat chain of command in blue. "But they had also attached several other units for support." She highlighted a smaller chain of command in gold.

Next she pulled out to a system wide map, and then circled a dot in space. "Logs from the sitrep show that most of the MEF had been lost with a research frigate 'Eli Whitney' in the local gas giant Gamma 7's gravity well, probably around when the Tactum fell. However, Dimitri and his squad of marines plus a trio of Spacer dropship pilots had been able to go hands-on and stay afloat. They had attempted rescue ops, like we did. Their ship not being rated for Gamma 7's corrosive atmosphere and the difference in tonnage meant that they never stood a chance. Their system log ends with Sergeant Volkov stating they would head for the FOB in Gamma 4."

"That would be a one-way trip, wouldn't it" Tai said.

Dax nodded. "Without a DS retriever module, or a carrier equipped for DS retrieval, they would be stuck on Gamma 4 for the duration."

"It paints a grim picture," Ramirez said. "Volkov's MEF element retreated to Gamma 4 and then found two things. One," she raised a finger, "something important enough to broadcast a general distress call, and two," she raised a second finger, "something dangerous enough to have to impede with a signal blocker."

"All in the locality of the one place in the solar system that we know will have the supplies for the Kyrie." Dax sighed another time. "I tell ya." He couldn't help but just shake his head. "What are the odds?"

"One," she raised her finger, "I am starting to strongly dislike it when you make overt references to poker and other games of luck." She raised a second finger. "Two, the odds are exactly one. It happened. This is obviously why you get into so much trouble gambling."

"I mean we have to go right? Even with the danger," Zeph said, his voice forlorn. "What's the alternative? Go planet to planet, system to system, just scavenging for the supplies we need for the next jump, barely surviving? With this—" his gesture took in the entire ship, "as the only sight we will ever see?" He stopped lowering is voice. "What kind of life is that," he said, barely above a whisper.

"It would be a life, eh," Abe said. "Not in the business end of a trap. Most likely murdered. All of us, our gear stolen. Or maybe they'll just rape and beat us, and then take our ship and strand us on a planet that is so backwater, I can smell the cow dung from here!"

Dax considered this. Grounding the Kyrie brought the grave and very likely probability of her never getting off planet. But not heading for the FOB meant a race between their life support and their reserve fuel.

"Abe," Dax said to private Ramadi, "I understand where you are coming from. Voids knows I always suspect everyone is out to shoot me. And I'm usually right." Before Tai could finish raising her eyebrow, however, he added, "Usually because I owe them money. But still, I understand expecting a brass knuckle in every backroom, a sidearm pointed at you from every shadow. But the law of the Void says that when there is a spacer in need, we must render aid if able." He paused a moment for, if he was being honest with himself, dramatic effect. "All we've get left in this galaxy is each other. I'd rather cling together for that warmth, instead of dying cold and alone in the void."

There weren't any claps afterwards, despite what Dax's extensive experience with holos would lead him to believe.

Ramirez, however, stepped up to save them from the awkward silence. "Okay, that's all nice and good, Captain, but when we get dirtside," she said, her Marine dropship slang coming out, "we are going to need a lot more than a vague plan and semi-inspirational speeches."

Semi. Ouch. Well, Dax deserved that. "What did you have in mind?"

"Clearly we have two objectives." Ramirez held up two fingers. "One, we need to recover Volkov's MEF element, or barring that, extract the data they discovered. As the Captain has stated, SOS calls are sacrosanct, especially one from one of our own." All the military person, active or otherwise, nodded. "Two, we need to locate supplies for the Kyrie. In fact, I probably should have made this point number one, but keeping the Kyrie operational should be of penultimate priority. Otherwise we are just another group of survivors needing rescue."

Dax turned to Bik. "She's really big into bullet points, huh?"

"She was part way through Officer Candidacy Training."

"That explains a lot." Dax remembered going through OCT on the suggestion of a commanding officer. But he realized his ass belonged in a pilot seat, not in an office chair.

Ramirez turned to glare at them. "Are you two completely finished?"

Dax gave her a thumbs-up, and Bik shrugged in the affirmative.

"Good. Two objectives demand two teams." She brought up a field mission display. "Team 1's objective is to recover the MEF element and investigate the satellite array." She circled the array and dragged two gold icons and one green "To that end, may I humbly suggest that we bring our best communication assets. Zeph, Abe, and myself in command."

She looked at Dax questioningly.

"No objections here," he said. "Like the saying goes, you have the flight, err field plan, you have the command."

"Good. Then team two, which will obviously be led by you, Captain, and consist of Tai, Kelly, and I hope you will take advise from Bik."

Dax turned to Bik and gave him a thumbs-up. He returned it with a shrug and a grin. He was making progress in communicating with the big man.

"And your objective is to perform recon on the FOB." She circled the FOB and brought two gold and two green tags on its perimeter. "And if Bik determines it is advisable to do so, retrieve the essential supplies." She turned to her marines, with Kelly facing the brunt of her glare. "Let's go easy on the shopping spree this time, okay?"

"Jeez, Sarge. The shopping spree is the only reason we all still alive and kicking," Kelly said, but still having the good grace to be embarrassed about it.

"With your consent, Captain, this is my suggested course of action."

Dax turned to Bik again. He cocked his head, and Bik shrugged in response. Dax clapped, followed by Zeph and Tai. "That OCT is really paying off."

"Quite," Zeph said.

"That's how you put together a plan, Cap," Tai said. "Take notes."

"Ooh, you wound me, Tai." Dax mimed a cut over his heart. "I make plans sometimes!"

"Does your plan," Tai asked, "involve 'barge in and shoot everything that wants to shoot us and hope for the best?'"

"You read my mind!"

"And what about peaceful negotiation and talks?" Tai asked, with Ramirez behind her, arms crossed arms and nodding.

"Well," Dax said, scratching his head, "we could try to shoot them all peaceful-like, but in my experience, that usually convinces them to shoot back in a non-peaceful-like manner."

Ramirez turned to Tai. "Does that ever work for him," Ramirez said, cocking a thumb at Dax. "The dirtside belt-miner accent and speak?"

"If by work you mean gets people to underestimate him, then most definitely no." Tai said, crossing her arms in her stern lecturing pose. "But if you mean get him into bar fights, then most definitely yes."

CHAPTER 21

Zeph keyed in the last sequence into his console. "I've got our approach vector spun up, Captain."

Dax nodded, and then thumbed his comm. "You may notice that the Captain, that's me, has turned on the fasten seatbelt sign."

"We're all good in here, Captain," Ramirez said. He could hear the wryness in her voice.

"In that case, thank you for joining us in Apocalypse Air. If you look out on your starboard side, you will see miles of pasture and farmland. And, for a special treat, if you look out port side, you will see miles of farmland and pasture.

"All right, hang onto your butts," Zeph said, "this is going to be rough." Rough was an understatement. Yes, Zeph had given them the most efficient approach vector to the planet, but with no Tactum powered orbital satellites to map out thermal deviations and air currents, it was the equivalent of doing heart surgery without nanocams: the risk of failure was high and the consequences fatal.

There was a subtle transition when they descended into Gamma 4's gravity well. Within a matter of moments, the Kyrie was no longer randomly spinning laterally but instead was in a corkscrew spin downwards. Into their doom. However, with the descent into the gravity well came a descent into the atmosphere of Gamma 4. Which meant Dax could make small hands-on changes by pointing the Kyrie into different angles of descent. But again, without the constant T-feed of atmospheric readings, it was like he was a nugget again, straining to read the dials and making the appropriate corrections.

It was a very delicate dance he performed, thousands of kilometers above the planet's surface. If angle of approach was too steep, he would never be able to decelerate enough to prevent the Kyrie from becoming a burning crater. But, if his angle of approach was too shallow, he would spend too much time in the upper atmosphere and become a burning meteorite instead. The trick was finding the sweet spot between the two fiery ends. He could feel it through the Kyrie's controls, however, before Zeph said anything.

"You're angled too low," Zeph said, grunting in his harness. "We're going in too fast."

"I know, I know," Dax said. He hated what he had to do

next, the precious resources from the Kyrie it would take. "Prepare for five second manual burn, on my mark."

Tai nodded, making the appropriate configuration changes. "Burn prep complete."

"Mark." The Kyrie burned irreplaceable fuel, retro thrusters firing, trying to angle her nose up from the steep angle she was currently. Trying to steer her from a fiery death. The marines in the bridge tensed in their seats. Unlike manning point defenses, exa-atmosphere approaches were not improved by more cooks in the kitchen.

"Burn complete" Tai said. "How are we reading, Zeph?"

"Uh . . ." Zeph looked at his console and plugged in some calculations. "Less dead, I'm pretty sure." He crunched more numbers. "But still a high chance of dead."

"There's always a high chance of dead," Dax said. But he could feel it in the vibrations of the Kyrie. These weren't the vibrations that would tear her apart. These were the vibrations that said she was stretching her wings and taking flight. "But I think we left the worst behind us."

"Technically above us," Zeph said, still tracking their angle of approach.

"No, I'm pretty sure the worst is still below us," Tai said, still being a grim realist.

"Well, one thing's for sure," Dax said. "Everyone on this planet has probably noticed our entry. Nothing we can do about it now. And at that point, the worst will be all around us."

A few hundred kilometers off the ground, Dax initiated another burn. Though it was necessary, he still resented the precious seconds of fuel. Based on the projected technological status of the planet, this might be a one-way trip for the Kyrie. It pained his heart to think of the Kyrie forever stranded dirtside on a planet instead of in space, free . . .

But with the last bursts of the retro thrusters, Kyrie gave a shudder and then settled into the ground.

"Successful landing," Zeph said, still reading mechanically off the readouts.

"Confirmed, nothing burned up in reentry," Tai said, the sarcasm lost on the astrogator.

"Good, very good." Zeph said.

"Dirtside, marines," Dax announced."

"Best news I've heard all day, Captain." Ramirez was probably glad that her marines could have a problem they could shoot at. Marines preferred very direct solutions.

"I'll be equalizing the cargo bay, so let's stage there before heading out."

Ramirez stood up from her inertia chair and shoulder her pack, gun slung across her chest. "Oscar Mike, marines!"

"And civilians," Tai added.

"Useful civilians," Ramirez said. With a nod. "Mission time start."

Mission time 0000.

CHAPTER 22

Mission time 0445

Dax hated it when he had a brilliant idea and no one listened to him.

"I told you we should have started with the 'bring guns' idea," Dax said. "They—" he emphasized the gunmen with a gesture, "obviously got the memo."

Both Bik and Tai remained silent, just glared at Dax.

Mission time 0125

Sunset over Gamma 4 was hauntingly beautiful. Gamma Solara minor lit an ocean of emerald that reached to the bloodred horizon and beyond, light refracting off the onyx black clouds in the distance. And the quiet. Without the Tactum, the legion of agri-drones remained still, and the only sound was the whirring of the local insectosoid. The humans were reticent to disturb the peace, buoyed by the gentle pace of the puma, Kyrie's cargo transport.

Bik sighed. "It reminds me of home. Chem green agri-crops, black carbon refractory clouds. Terraformed of course, just like my home planet. It was the Tribe Chiefs themselves that sold our land and our people to slavery. The Cooperative's offers for subsidization were too substantial to pass up." He looked towards the sunset, and sighed. "My peoples were given a chance to be free, but given the prerogative, they chose servitude for themselves. At least my colony did." He shrugged and patted his machine gun.

Tai and Dax stared at the oft quiet marine, surprised by the most consecutive words he had uttered since they met.

"Feeling homesick, Bik?" Kelly asked.

Bik chuckled to himself. "Hardly, Kelly." He took a deep breath, seeming to savor the air around him. "While I hold a tiny longing for my tribe, it is my home that is sick of me." He smiled and shook himself out of his reverie. "No, just trying to work up the strength to break this beautiful peace." He reluctantly picked up the radio. "Sergeant, this is Mbikala, come in." The man spoke over the radio with a clear, refined accent.

They had decided to check in every fifteen minutes mission time and to use the marines' shortwave radio instead of their wristcoms. Just in case hostile elements were scanning burst transmissions. Or even not-hostile-but-opportunistically-in-a-thieving-mood elements were scanning in the area.

"I read you Bik, what do you got for me?" Ramirez's voice came in with just a hint of static. They were close to the radio's optimal distance.

"We will soon reach the base's perimeter, but our sweeps look clear. We are going to proceed."

"With caution, of course."

"Of course."

There was a moment of silence. "Have the Captain copy on that."

Bik turned to look at Dax, raising one eyebrow quizzically at him.

Dax grabbed the set from Bik's hand. "That's a low blow, Ramirez."

There was an audible sigh from her end. "That isn't a copy."

"Yes, yes, copy Sergeant." Dax returned the set to Bik. "Let's get this done. 'With caution' all right? An extra helping of it. Over and out."

Bik just shrugged, smiled, and embraced the silence once again.

Mission time 0315

"Check in, Specialist Mbikala."

"Copy, Sergeant. We have discovered the cell depot and are stocking up now." They had found the depot near the center of the base. It was a large gray durasteel structure with a large roll up doors. Thankfully Bik's ID had let them key into the side entrance.

"That's good. Captain, how are the Kyrie's armament's doing?"

Dax leaned in around Bik. "I've had Tai dealing with logistics on that. She trying to optimize our storage capacity volume between fuel cells, energy cells, and nano-block ammunition." He pressed the blister on his wristcom to page Tai. Nothing happened.

"Tai, come over, where—"

Tai came up behind him, her wristcom displaying a logistics list for the Kyrie.

"Why aren't you answering your comm?" Dax asked.

Tai tapped her ear. "These aren't going to work without a transmitter. We had these slaved to the Kyrie's emitter, remember?"

"Oh yeah…well the Sergeant is asking how the resupply is going."

Tai's face actually lit up. "It's like lunar new year in here, but every red envelope I open has ammunition instead of money in it!" She gave a laugh that trailed off in the end. "Well, it's the end of the world so I guess money isn't worth anything." She shrugged, open another crate and showed it to Dax. "Look, nano-block."

"That's good. Thank goodness your point defense uses nano-block instead of traditional rounds," Ramirez said over the radio. Nano-block was depleted fissile mass with, as the name suggested, nanobots. The macroscopic bots would key in to the weapons ammunition signature and form the right caliber and type.

"And as a bonus," Dax said, "if we run into anymore killer ninja robots, the sidearm I'm carrying this time is modded to load nano-block as well and your weapons are standard energy cell, so we can economize on the space."

There was a pause before Ramirez spoke again. "Isn't nano-block mods for civilian firearms illegal?"

Dax gave Bik an apologetic grin before responding. "Well, you see, I might have claimed to still be active military when I had it modded back in Beta so . . ."

"Captain, was there anything above board with your transport business venture?"

"Space pirates," Dax said, the same time Tai said, "Well our Ring visas were legitimate."

"Only because those are voiding impossible to forge," Dax said, while Tai offloaded a crate of nano blocks on the puma's cargo bay. "And we would know, we went to the best laser forgers in Pi." Dax gave Tai a quick hand before returning to speak over Bik's shoulder. "We would have tried to use Tai's connections in the inner system to get closer to the source, but I'm pretty sure there is an imperial decree about forging Ring visas."

"Execution," Tai said.

"Yes, that," Dax said.

"Why would Tai...you know, I don't want to know," came Ramirez's voice over the radio. "End of the world and all of that."

"Hey, ya'll just gonna sit there yapping and making all the ladies do all the work?" Kelly said, hauling a pallet of fuel cells.

"Sergeant, how goes things on your end?" Bik said, then clipping the set on his bandolier and helping Private Kelly.

"Zeph and Abe were finally able to tap into the array's security," Ramirez said.

"Is that Dax?" came Zeph's voice over the radio. "Tell him and Tai that just like the original signal, I had to use a cascading reversal algorithm—"

"Needless to say, your Astrogator has been immense help," Ramirez said. "The main console has been locked from public access, so the two of them have been working on gaining aces on that. Check-in in a quarter again, okay Bik?"

"Copy, Sergeant, over and out." Bik double clicked his set and went back to hauling.

Kelly looked at Tai and Dax. "Pirates," she said, and just shook her head.

"Space Pirates," Tai and Dax said in unison.

Mission time 0445

Dax was thinking, once it was time to leave, that events had been transpiring rather smoothly and that they were overdue a catastrophic event. Tai had calculated max load for the puma, with just enough wiggle room for the rest of them. So naturally it was when they left the depot that things went sideways.

They had only gone a few meters past the base's front perimeter exit when they came upon a thresher drone blocking their path.

"Tai, refresh my memory here real quick, but that was definitely not there before, correct?"

Tai gave him a grim look. "Most definitely not."

Bik's radio squawked. "Bik, Captain, we've decrypted the message. The signal they are trying to block—"

The thresher drone came to life. "Voids!" Dax said, as he unholstered his sidearm. "Get us out of here! Bik, Kelly, watch out for . . ." The words died in his mouth as several thresher and reaper drones descended from the sky. Had they been hiding in the carbon clouds?

When they were a few feet from the air, armed men hopped off from their backs, and pointed weapons at the occupants of the puma.

"I told you we should have started with the 'bring guns' idea," Dax said. "They—" he emphasized the gunmen with a gesture, "obviously got the memo."

Both Bik and Tai remained silent, just glared at Dax.

Mission Time 0530

"That thing is most definitely interfering with our radio

signal," Tai said, looking sideways towards Dax from where she kneeled, hands tied behind her back.

"It leads from the logic of our circumstance," Bik said, similarly tied and kneeling like Tai. "It explains why our radio signal cut off and why we have not heard the Sergeant since."

Knowing Ramirez, she should have been squawking on the set demanding a sitrep and why they missed the last two check-ins. Dax looked at his wristcom display. Last three check-ins. "What is that thing is the real mystery."

The thing in question had been a harvester rover. Had being the operative phrase. But it had since been retrofitted with a bristle array of antennas and dishes.

"What did Abe say," Tai said, her voice a hoarse whisper. "Ad hoc something or another."

"You know I stop listening when he speaks tech juju," Dax said.

"Ad hoc transmitter acting as drone controller," Bik said.

A man stepped out of the harvester rover cum drone controller and approached them.

"Voids," Dax said, wishing he was untied and standing. "Time to face the wizard behind the curtain." And while he was wishing, it would be nice to have his sidearm back. At least in the scramble, Kelly had been able to escape their captors.

With Gamma 4's sun down, the immense plain was lit only by the lights of the assembled drones and vehicles.

The figure approached them, but stayed out of the light, remaining shrouded in darkness. "Welcome to Gamma 4," said the figure. "We apologize for the overtly hostile gesture, but you did enter our atmosphere unannounced and good intentions are in short supply."

"What if we told you are intentions are peaceful?" Dax asked. "Would you release us then?"

"Alas, that cannot be so." The figure's voice was tinged with authentic regret. "Because, unfortunately, you have already proven yourself at cross purpose to ours."

Dax, Tai, and Bik shared a confused look among themselves.

"Look, we do apologize for the lack of a proper declaration and inquiry of entry, but unfortunately our shortwave communications were damaged, and the T-transmitter—" Dax paused.

"Yes, I understand. But that is not our qualm with your presence."

"Well, that's sure a change of pace. Most people have qualms with my mere presence," Dax said, testing the room. "But if not that, then what?"

The figure approached them, bringing himself into the light. He was of average stature for a person raised in standard gravity. But he carried himself in a stately and refined manner.

He went up to Bik, and forced him to look up, Bik's muscles straining against his restraints. "You, marine."

"Specialist Jean-Gerard Mbikala, OCM—" Bik started.

'Yes, yes, OCMC." He examined the OCMC seal on Bik's lapel. "I am not interested in your rank nor serial number. I am interested in this." He roughly grabbed Bik's wrist and twisted.

A gold holo tag appeared before them, initiated by the blister that the man was depressing. "This got you into the FOB, did it not?"

"We will not arm your twisted band of murder bots," Dax said.

Tai groaned quietly at murder bots, but Dax was enraged.

"Weapons? What need have I for weapons?" With some unseen command, the figure brought a drone in, its wicked reaper arm threateningly close to Dax and his team. "My swarm is weapon enough." He pet the drone fondly.

"No, I have no need for access to the FOB. But I do wonder if this will likewise grant you access to the military communications facility on this planet.

Dax and Tai stiffened involuntarily.

"So, this is not unknown to you," the figure said, his face framed in harsh light as he inspected them each in turn. "In fact, I posit that this facility is part and parcel to why you are here." He released Bik's wrist. "I will use your access, with or without your live bodies attached to them, to get what I need to leave this dirty backside of a planet."

Dax was relieved. This person assumed that they had not

yet got access to the array. But there was still the very large possibility that he would kill them anyway when he found out.

The figure took a step back and tapped on his wristcom. Several drones lifted into the air and circled him, casting their lights as spotlights onto him. "You may call me Valentin." His gesture took in the great expanse of darkness surrounding them. "All that is left in this galaxy, is me. I will do what I must to stay whole, even if I must take from others. There is no more law. There is only survival."

It upset Dax that Valentin's speech was like a perverse mirror of his own, but that his presentation was definitely more impressive.

CHAPTER 23

The silhouette of the communication facility stood as an imposing skyline, piercing the heavens above it.

Dax broke in with a curse. "Holy mother of—"

"Language," Tai said in warning.

"—communication arrays." He finished. He was prepared for big. He had not been prepared for monolithic.

"It is impressive, to say the least." Valentin nodded towards the structure. "It pings in the Exahertz range, or so I have been told by our technicians."

Tai and Bik nodded.

"Oh yeah, Exahertz, hmmm yes," Dax said, not wanting to be left out.

Valentin grinned. He was an older man, his hair and beard graying, but regal. And he spoke in a captivating and charismatic way. Dax found himself having to resist its seductive appeal. "You can pick up the dying breaths of a star collapsing into a black hole with that sensitivity." His face grew grim. "Or send a command signal that could span the entire system."

Tai narrowed her eyes. "So that's why."

Dax was lost, but he decided to play to his strengths: He pretended to know what he was talking about. "Yeah, we're on to you, Valentin."

"Obviously," Valentin said. "It's not like I was trying to hide it. What else was I to do? A whole army of now unregistered T-drones. And a whole solar system with nobody to stand up against me."

They approached the Satellite array in convo, Valentin's rover taking point, their puma, still supply laden, in the middle, with a small army of thresher and reaper drones surrounding them. Obviously Valentin was a gifted drone controller, despite having to use a non-ideal control method. The drones moved organically, like a living swarm.

Bik said one word. "Parolee."

"Yes, that is what they called me." He displayed a black colored ID tag from his wristcom. "Just a cleaner word for 'slave,' isn't it?"

His tag had three red slashes running across it. "A fitting prison then, for a serial murderer," Tai said. "They did the galaxy a service by paroling you to work the agri-fields."

Valentin turned to them, a strange expression on his face.

"Work. Ha." He brought a droid closer and, without looking, stepped off the puma, landing lightly on the drone's upper canopy. "Quickly was I given 'privilege' when the controllers discovered my aptitude for drone heuristics. They were happy, no ecstatic to give me more 'privilege.' I was free labor after all." With the controls on his wristcom, he gracefully circled the puma and Dax's team.

"And free labor doing the work of skilled technicians just made for a better bottom line." He brought the drone to a relative stop just above and ahead of them. "Maybe if those skilled technicians had known their job better, it would be them, not I, who would have had the 'privilege' of ripping the other limb by limb." He stepped off the drone and then fondly patted it before sending it off to rejoin the swarm. "Irony, then: A slave rising up with other slaves to overcome their shared task-masters."

He gave another bombastic sweeping gesture that included everything before him. "I was not destined to work. I was destined to conquer."

Dax was slow, but he had caught up by now. He considered that, while there were those who felt the end of the galaxy meant holding on to that unspoken law of spacers and humanity, there were others who saw the end as a release from bondage. Release from the tethers of law, government, a social code of ethics. The end meant there were no longer any chains. Or it meant that someone else could hold the chains.

"Why?" Dax asked.

"Gamma 3 is where the rich and fat live. Yes, the slave masters deserved to die at the hands of my children." Darkness crossed Valentin's face. "But even more so the apparatchiks of the corporate machine." A smile spread across his face, as he turned to face them again. "Imagine the irony, the sweetest of its kind, when those that ruled with a technological iron first are instead enslaved by my swarm." He licked his lips obscenely. "They shall become my parolees. Sweetest of ironies indeed."

Dax didn't know what to say. So, in a rare instance in his life, he said nothing at all.

They reached the satellite array facility when Valentin turned to Dax. "I heard them call you captain. Enlighten me, how many are in your crew?"

Dax tensed. "Three. Only three of us."

Valentin grinned "Surely you meant four. Your companion who escaped?"

He grimaced. "Yes, four, of course. Only four."

Valentin stroked his beard, contemplating. He stepped off the puma, landing again on a drone. Whether the same or different, Dax could not tell. Then, they were all lifted by the arms of three reaper drones and brought towards the secure entrance of the facility.

At the entrance, they were lined up in front of Valentin and his small crew of human ex-parolees. Valentin sent the swarm to circle them, vultures circling a carcass.

"I think," Valentin said, commanding the drone to drop Bik to his knees, "that there are more of your crew here." He pulled out a sidearm. "Much more. And I think the rest of them are ensconced in this facility."

He depressed Bik's radio set. "Hello, this Parolee 24601, Vincent Valentin. You have five minutes to open these doors and grant us access to the array's main control center or I will maim this marine, one specialist Jean-Gerard Mbikala." He placed the barrel against Bik's jugular. "Not to kill, mind you. Just gravely injure. So you can have the privilege of listening to him slowly die."

CHAPTER 24

Dax was getting real tired of people pointing guns at him and his crew.

"I don't know how your people did it," Valentine said, "but they cracked the encryption, didn't they?"

Dax swore to himself that the next time, he would be doing the gun pointing, mark his words. Instead he was here, at the edge of civilization, staring down a megalomaniac with a ninja murderbot army, and nothing to shoot with.

"If you cracked it, that means you can disable that filter that the pesky marine put on my off-world transmissions." Valentin looked at his wristcom timer. "Five minutes."

"I just want to make sure I am hearing you correctly," Tai said. "I thought this was about rising against your oppressors. We have not oppressed you."

"At some point, I realized that I was given this," he

gestured to parolees who trailed him like rabid dogs, the drones that moved at his command, the entire planet, "all of this, for a reason. I deserved it," he said, his voice wistful. "All I had to do was reach out," he stretched out his open hand, "and take it." He violently closed his hand into a fist. "And anything that stood in my way was oppressing my right." He smiled at them. What scared Dax the most was Valentin's eyes. They were not crazed, or wild, or desperate. They were calm, clear, and seductive. "Two minutes."

Tai looked at Dax and grinned. "So, you and your ten boys decided to form a lynch mob." Tai said, her tone almost robotic. "I figured you'd wait until two o'clock first before rolling out the welcome wagon and then feed us supper at seven."

Dax looked at Tai, confused. But Valentin didn't miss a beat.

"Call it what you want. I care not," Valentin said. "I have been in this life longer than my life as a Cooperative citizen. For what, the lives of three children? I will take the lives of their children in payment." He pressed the barrel harder against Bik's neck, for emphasis. "One minute."

"Sounds like a lot of hot air blowing to me," Tai said, pointing three fingers into a random direction. "What did you offer your sick hanger-ons? Did you promise them glory? Pillage and the spoils of war? A pet slave to call their own?"

"They are here because they know to follow strength,"

Valentin said. His pose stood around them, stone-faced. "I offered all the parolees the same choice I will offer you: freedom from bondage or allegiance to me. The parolees that chose allegiance stand here and elsewhere, smaller hives at their control. The others, I gave freedom from the bondage of their frail bodies." He shrugged and grinned at Tai "thirty seconds."

"Well," Tai said. "That sounds like a solid plan as any. When do we start?"

Valentin looked quizzically at Tai. "Why, little girl, we have already begun. I will get into this facility. Whether you will be alive to see it is your prerogative." "

Tai looked at Valentin, murder in her eyes. Dax tensed, readying himself. She opened her mouth. "I'm ready to try my luck if you are."

"Zero minutes."

A shot cracked the sky. Tai dove. And all hell broke loose.

CHAPTER 25

Kelly had grown up shooting and ranching. While she enjoyed the ranching, she was a natural at the shooting. She had been two weeks away from submitting her paperwork for marksmen quals, but she figured this right here would prove whether or not she had what it took to be a combat shooter.

She spoke through her comm headpiece.

"Tai, give me confirmation you can hear me five-by-five."

"I just want to make sure I am hearing you correctly," Tai said in response. She saw Tai staring down Valentin from over 500 yards out through her rifle scope.

"That damn snake oil bastard. I guess Abe was right, and he's just going to be insufferable about it."

"I thought this was about rising against your oppressors. We have not oppressed you." Tai said.

"Wow he does like to hear himself speak. Like someone else I know." Kelly watched Tai look at Dax and grin. "Tai, can you give me a count? I want to make sure I am not missing any."

"So," Tai said, "you and your ten boys decided to form a lynch mob."

"Good. I count ten as well. Which one confiscated your sub compact?"

"I figured you'd wait until two o'clock first before rolling out the welcome wagon, and then feed us supper at seven."

"Your two o'clock and seven o'clock. Roger. Can you get me a wind reading down there? You all are bunched up real tight, and I don't want to miss."

"Sounds like a lot of hot air blowing to me," Tai said. She pointed three fingers at South West.

Three centimeters per second due 233 degrees southwest. She adjusted her rangefinder to compensate.

"Give me a bit of time, I have to tighten up the readings on my scope here."

"What did you offer your sick hanger-ons? Did you promise them glory? Pillage and the spoils of war? A pet slave to call their own?" Tai asked, ramping up the drama in her voice.

"Okay, maybe a little too much drama." Kelly did the range math. Without a spotter, things were going to get hairy. "I'm going to disarm the folks holding your weapons, and then ya'll better get real twisty like."

"Well," Tai said. "That sounds like a solid plan as any. When do we start?"

"On my mark," Kelly said, bracing her left hand against the rifle.

"I'm ready to try my luck if you are."

Kelly fired.

CHAPTER 26

Dax saw the first shot hit the man right in front of Tai, the one holding her subcompact. She dove into a crouch and caught the gun, and from her position, reached out with a swipe and downed another. She flipped over the man's body and used it as cover as she started firing at the others.

The second shot hit the man holding Dax's sidearm. He dove for it, but he lacked the natural grace that Tai had. He made up the difference in quality with quantity. Of bullets.

Valentin had fled for cover, freeing up Bik. The big but unarmed marine headbutted the man nearest him.

"What is happening?" Dax yelled. "Who is shooting?"

Tai looked at him. "What? It's Kelly? Didn't you hear us over the comms?"

"What, comms are back? I turned them off when you

told me—" he pressed the blister on his wristcom. The whole squad was there, Ramirez loudly directing them.

"You didn't know the entire time?" Ramirez asked over comms, incredulous. "But how did you know the signal?"

"Signals are more your thing," Dax said. He shot at a drone to down it. Out. He flicked his wrist and speed-reloaded a nano-block into the sidearm's chambers. "Shooting and asking why later is more my thing."

Kelly was still firing as well, covering Tai and Dax's blind spots as they engaged the close quarter elements. Tai was a ballet of destruction. She was fast, agile, and a joy to watch. She took a drone down with a burst to control matrix, then rolled and pivoted and struck another with the butt of her subcompact to give her more space and stun its gyroscopic stabilizer. Tai fought like an art form.

Dax fought in the way he knew best, like bar brawl in the middle of happy hour. Dax was rapid firing from the hip, and wrestling with thresher arms between reloads. And like a bar brawl, he spent a lot of that time on the ground, covered in dirt.

"Damnit," Kelly cursed.

"Language," Dax said, looking around.

"Every time I take a clear shot at Valentin," Kelly said, "a drone comes swooping in, taking the bullet for him." She cursed again. "I think I just made him angry. It's going to get hot on me soon. What do you think it is?"

"Some sort of proximal velocity algorithm?" Zeph said. "I mean, it's possible."

"I'm going to test it," Dax said. He kicked the nearest drone's arm, keeping it away from his chest, and rolled underneath it and took aim at Valentin. He fired six shots in rapid succession. The nearest drone preempted each shot. "He has something."

"Did you see him touch his wristcom?" Zeph asked

"No, he wasn't even looking at me. I'm pretty sure he's sending drones out to look for Kelly." Dax grunted, narrowly avoiding the reaper blade of a drone. "Watch your six."

There was one more high caliber shot. Dax looked behind him. Kelly had taken out the optics on the drone that had snuck up behind him.

"Repositioning," said Kelly's calm voice over the comm. "T minus fifteen seconds before overwatch is back on angels."

Bik roared triumphantly. He had retrieved his machine gun from the Puma. The handful of drones left wouldn't stand a chance. He let loose a withering hail of bullets.

Dax looked for Valentin, but he was nowhere to be found. "Does anyone have eyes on—wait," Dax said in realization. "If we have comms back, that means . . ."

"Kelly, Kyrie is inbound from your north, northwest." Ramirez said over the comm. "She will be coming in hot! Repeat, Kyrie in bound." Dax smiled.

Bik laughed. He had just downed the last drone, the rest

were fleeing.

"Go back to where you came from, yah filthy animals, Dax said and whooped.

"By the voids," Tai cursed. He turned to her, and then looked at where she was pointing.

"Is that . . ." Dax squinted at the horizon. "Clouds?"

Tai shook her head.

It looked like clouds rolling in loaded with hail. It looked like a flock of birds. It looked like…"A swarm," he said. Dax groaned.

"Uh guys, I'm in a bit of a pickle here," Kelly said.

Dax looked from the swarm, to the array station, to the puma, to the little black dot on the horizon that was the Kyrie. "Guys, I have a plan."

"Let's hear this plan," Ramirez said.

CHAPTER 27

"I take back the part where I called this a plan," Ramirez said. Understandably she had qualms about the sequence of events that Dax had put forth, either in their sequence or the said events themselves.

"Look," Dax said, "it's not like we have a lot of choices left before us, in lieu of the literal army of murder ninja bots."

"If there was a name for a thing that was the opposite of a plan, it would be this thing."

"Now you are just trying to hurt my feelings, Ramirez."

Dax could hear her throw her hands up in disgust. "Let's do this."

He turned to Tai and Bik and gave them a thumbs-up. They both shook their heads but didn't utter a word in complaint. They were hunkered down behind the Puma.

"Tai do you have eyes on Valentin?" Dax flicked the

sidearm's chamber open and grabbed a fresh block with his off hand.

Tai shook her head. "He took the remaining parolees and drones, and his harvester, and was heading for the main swarm."

Bik looked at Dax. No...he looked at Dax's hands.

"You do that with much skill," Bik said, and whistled.

Tai smiled. "He spends a lot of time shooting and getting shot."

Dax gave a wide grin, and flicked his wrist once more, closing the chamber. "So, you all want to shoot them all peaceful-like?"

They all jumped into the puma, Bik in the driver's seat, while Tai and Dax buckled in and pulled up their wristcom displays.

"Zeph, you ready for this?" Dax asked.

"No," Zeph said, "but Kelly is about to get ripped apart limb by limb soon . . ."

"Pretty damn soon!" Kelly said, out of breath.

"Captain, I am slaving controls now," Abe said.

"Initiating beacon sequence," Zeph said.

Dax was jostled roughly as Bik drove them almost haphazardly to Kelly's position, where she was about to be overtaken by drones. On his comm display he had the Kyrie's instrument panel. And nothing else. He could see the Kyrie, coming in hot from the north-northwest, but between them and her was a horde of agri-drones hell bent on devouring them, all of them converging on the private.

"You hands-on, Cap, Tai?" Abe asked.

"Yes." they both said. Complete focus. Complete trust.

"Handing over controls to you."

Dax was now remotely controlling the Kyrie's flight systems while Tai was on weapons.

"I don't got much left in these magazines, Cap," Tai said, a grim expression on her face.

"We don't need much, just enough." Dax was weaving the Kyrie through the mass, using proximity readings to guess the direction of the incoming drones. He was impressed. The swarm was composed of hundreds of drones, from his best guess, but they moved like one organism.

While he banked and rolled, Tai was firing the point defense guns, keeping the swarm at bay.

"Distance?" Dax said, sparing just a little concentration away from his controls.

"I am approaching Kelly's ID sensor," Bik said.

"There's a lot of interference," Abe said, "but the beacon is starting to get through."

Dax gritted his teeth. Just a little more. Every loop and dip was a dance step. Closer and closer he circled, ever approaching the vortex of the swarm. The eye of the storm that now circled on Kelly.

"We're almost there, Kelly. Ramirez, you ready?" Dax

asked.

"I think I'm going to be sick," Ramirez said, but voice still stoic.

"I'm sorry there aren't any inertia chairs in the cargo bay, we moved them all to the bridge to accommodate you all—"

"That's fine, that's fine. You sure you can do this?" Ramirez asked.

"She's a retired drop ship," Dax said, prepping his controls. "And I'm a retired drop ship pilot."

"Okay, I trust you," Ramirez said. "As long as you stop saying 'retired' over and over—"

"Guys, not to be downer here," Kelly said, a tinge of hysteria in her voice, "but I did say pickle, y'all."

They hit a particularly hard bump that made Bik grunt. "We are almost to your position, Kelly."

"Mags dry, Cap," Tai said, throwing her arms up in frustration.

"I'm going for the split S!" Dax inverted the Kyrie and then pulled her into a half loop, giving up altitude for speed. The swarm dove to follow. When she was parallel to the ground, Dax spun the Kyrie laterally, converting her downward momentum into rotational. Some of the drones couldn't recover fast enough and they smashed into the ground.

Dax expelled virtually all their remaining fuel cells on retro thrusters, neutralizing the lateral spin. He opened the cargo bay.

"Guys!" Kelly screamed.

Ramirez jumped out of the Kyrie's bay before the door fully dropped. She was in Tai's hardsuit to compensate for some of the g-forces. She landed on a thresher drone that was moments away from harvesting Kelly. She placed the shotgun on the upper canopy and pulled the trigger.

The drone's internal circuitry exploded out of it, falling to the ground.

She hopped from its remains and landed on the ground, rolling to compensate. She pulled out of the roll and whipped her shotgun out to take point-blank aim at the next closest drone to Kelly. When it fell, it revealed the sweaty panicked face of the private.

Ramirez reached behind her back and tossed Kelly her rifle. The private caught it and formed back-to-back with the sergeant, driving back the swarm temporarily.

"Abe, Zeph, about now would be wonderful," Dax said as they approached the two marines.

"Beacon's tone is good!" Abe said, just as Kelly and Ramirez jumped into the puma. They drove it up the cargo door ramp and into the belly of the Kyrie.

Bik quickly dismounted and roared his machine gun to life, firing out of the open bay trying to keep the swarm from swallowing up the Kyrie from the inside out.

Dax was dry. He reached for another nano-block on his

bandolier. His hand came back empty.

"By the voids, it's now or nev—"

"Now!" Zeph said.

The handful of drones closest to the Kyrie shuddered, one of them with a thresher arm that was still extended about to impale Tai.

Zeph gave a whoop over the comm. Those drones turned and flew at their ex-compatriots.

Metal clashed against metal in pained moans and squeals. Each time a defected drone was destroyed, Zeph attenuated the beacon frequency to take over another. They fought the impending wave to a standstill.

Then they started overtaking it.

"Sequence decrypted," Abe said.

The swarm consumed itself.

They landed the Kyrie a few meters from the array. In fact, they parked next to the shredded remains of Valentin's drone controller slash harvester. He and the remaining parolees were being restrained by drones, feet bound together and arms spread wide.

Abe and Zeph exited the array and met the rest of the crew. They were all in one piece, mostly. Kelly had a long gash along her chest but nothing cycle in the med bay wouldn't fix. Ramirez was a little green in gills, but then, she had experienced several g's worth of evasive maneuvers. Even with a drop suit.

Valentin looked up at them as they approached, barely concealing the rage painted on his face. He spat in their direction and uttered only one word. "How."

Abe responded. "The drones were protecting you from our bullets," he said. "Which meant that you had programmed them with some defensive heuristic. That meant that they could override your hands-on control if they needed to sacrifice themselves for you."

Valentin just glared at them as he sat there, pinned up by the remains of his own swarm.

"Which means," Zeph said from Abe's side, "that you programmed an override. All we had to do was access that program. Which was not an easy feat without the Tactum. But you already knew that." Zeph gestured to the array. "We couldn't penetrate your signal with the array, because that's what was preventing your signal from going planetwide."

"But we had transmitter beacons on the Kyrie, and the Kyrie has tight beam so when Bik stopped checking in, Ramirez humped it to the Kyrie and . . ." Zeph shrugged sheepishly. "It's all very complicated programming work after that. I don't want to burden you with the details."

Bik spoke up. "So in the end, you were just another taskmaster whose slaves rose up against him."

Valentin looked at each them in kind. "Kill me."

"Oh no," Dax said. "I mean, I'll shoot someone in a stand-up gun fight, in defense of me and mine, but I don't kill in cold blood like some people, present company included."

Tai approached Valentin and crossed her arms. "Well Tai has been known to get violent with those who threaten me with harm," Dax said. She raised an eyebrow in agreement.

Ramirez levelled the barrel of her shotgun at Valentin. "I will admit," Dax said, "I'm not too sure about her."

"I will adhere to the uniform code of Cooperative justice here," she said. "Even if you have the blood of marines on your hands." Her voice dropped to a menacing pitch. "We won't kill you, but you will wish we had." She smiled. It was cold and it did not reach her eyes. Instead she pulled up her wrist comm, displaying the collection of gold ID tags that did make her eyes glitter metallically. With a gesture, she pulled another group of gold tags into her collection. One proudly displayed "SGT Dimitri Ivanovich Volkov, OCMC-MEF".

Dax figured that she, and all the marines, had lost the most so far. And Ramirez carried those losses with her. On her wrist. In her soul.

"But no, if there is no discipline, then I can no longer stand for the Corp. Semper Fidelis. Always faithful, eh?" She smiled. "In times of war, we would treat you as a prisoner of war and send you to headquarters to be detained by the military police."

She paused. Valentin grinned.

"Well that is a problem, isn't it?" He said.

"Yes, because I know no headquarters or detainment facility to remand you to." Her words were sharp enough to cut. "But I think will honor the spirit of Sergeant Volkov in this way."

Dusk was settling once again on the plains of Gamma 4, the painfully beautiful sunset being painted across the sky. There was a stillness as a breeze rippled the knee-high grass. Strewn along the ground, the corpses of dismembered drones lay inert, and in their center were survivors of the galaxy-wide end.

Some survivors chose to draw closer, some survivors chose to render asunder. Dax wondered if it was this catastrophic on other planets, other systems. Were lines drawn between those who held onto their humanity and those who discarded it? Could the humane contain the cruel?

"Volkov wanted to make sure you never left this planet to reign your terror on others." Ramirez looked Valentin in the eye. "But one thing he did not have was a skilled programmer."

Zeph winked. "Good luck trying to pass commands to the new bios I uploaded to the drones planet-wide." Zeph tapped his chin. "I mean, I'm sure you will figure it out, with time, but then, so will the others."

Valentin looked up, sharply. "Others?"

"Oh, I guess you couldn't tell," Abe said. "No way to communicate long distances and all. Others survived on other plantation sites. And this time, instead of static, the entire planet, hey the entire solar system, knows of your crimes. They'll come for you, eventually. Survival means taking from others, isn't that right?"

"Irony," Dax said. "Or is that appropriateness? I always got those two mixed up." He turned to Ramirez and gestured to the Kyrie. "Boots star-side, Marines."

And with that, the crew of the Kyrie embarked.

CHAPTER 28

"How is she doing on fuel, Zeph?" Dax asked the moment he got into the command desk.

"PFCs are loaded, but they will need a few cycles to—"

"Uh Cap," Abe said. "You are going to want to take a look at this." He slid something over from his screen and threw it up on the main console. Valentine's wristcom was transmitting, but in shortwave tight beam only.

"What am I looking at?" Dax asked. "More drone protocol?"

"No way he could have decrypted my bios," Zeph said, checking his.

"That is a remote protocol," Ramirez said. "But it's not drone protocol."

"What is it then?" Tai asked, worry coloring her tone.

"Remote missile protocol."

Everyone looked at their screens, trying to figure out what possible threat they could be facing.

Tai found it first. "I am detecting multiple surface to sub orbital missiles being launched."

"What the voids? Can we juke 'em?" Dax asked, jumping into his inertia chair and strapping himself in.

"I mean, we barely have enough fuel to evade one, let alone the six I'm counting," Tai said.

"Seven," Ramirez said. "One was in the radar shadow of the mountains."

"I need options!" Dax was hands-on again.

"Our counter measures are not that effective in atmo," Abe said.

"And the effective range of our guns is exceeded by the blast radius of those SSOMs," added Bik.

"Ohwowow my goodness, I can't believe I'm saying this." Zeph rubbed his face furiously before continuing. "Boss, I can spin up a blind jump."

"I don't know Zeph, once was already pushing our luck… but twice in one apocalypse?"

"'A probability of dying in the other side of the solar system is a heck of a lot better odds than the surety of dying on this side?'

Dax paused. "You cheeky son of a full house. Do it!"

Zeph keyed up jump coordinates.

"Uh Zeph," Abe said. "What is this spinning up?"

"That's strange, it's the Nav module spinning up." Zeph looked really confused.

"The what?" Dax asked.

"And it's establishing a T-network." Zeph said.

"The how?"

"It's processing the jump algorithm in real time." Zeph's eyes were about to pop out of his eyes.

"The when?"

"The Nav module we download from the comm station. You know, the thing Volkov asked us to retrieve? It seems to be linking up with the navigation computer through Tactum interface and—" before Dax could finish, Zeph's console, the one housing the said module, exploded into a sea of lights.

And the Kyrie jumped

PART THREE
PINNACLE

CHAPTER 29

A thick miasma of silence hung in the recycled air of the Kyrie's cabin.

It was amidst this silence that Ramirez spoke the obvious.

"So, now that we've thrown ourselves into the maw of the void, and ignoring the fact that the Tactum WORKS in here for some magical reason—What. In. The. Void. Am I looking at?" Through their viewport they could see a shimmering blue surface. The event horizon of the Ring. It had been active before they even approached it.

The outburst broke the stasis and Dax and the crew huddled around Zeph's display, the orange glow of the holo casting eerie shapes on the stark faces.

"It's a rally beacon. Or at least, I thought that's all it was," Abe said. "It had the standard Our Cooperative Armed Forces signature for a rally beacon."

"This is what you found in the array?" Dax asked. Dax was slightly miffed that while he had been held prisoner by a sadistic serial killer, Zeph and Abe had been doing silly computer things. He consoled himself that he had been able to shoot things, however.

"No, this is just what Volkov left behind." Zeph then pulled up an astral map and threw it on the main display. "The array, however, found a spatial anomaly with the Ring space."

"I thought the entirety of Ring space was an anomaly," Dax said. "I feel like you are telling me you found a drop of water in an ocean."

"Okay, um." Zeph scratched his head, and then rotated the astral map to a certain view. "So tetra voids, right, that's bad. Like real bad."

Dax shivered. Even with his limited astrography, he knew that more than bad. "Eigenvalues zero, dot zero, dot zero, dot zero."

"Exactly, where all radical formations converge, resulting in…well you know…death." Zeph said. "Uncertainty principle and all of that."

"Uh," Abe said, "English? Errr…astro-English at least?"

"Sure, sure." Zeph bit his lip. "I mean, I am just going to mangle a bunch of theoretical astrophysics here."

"Of course," Dax said nonchalantly. "Wouldn't have it any other way."

"The reason we can travel through the Ring space almost instantaneously is the same reason we can't traverse around the Ring space. In there, all four dimensions exist, like in our space, but in the Ring space we can travel by constraining the time dimension. It's the only thing that doesn't obey relativistic laws."

"Uh, English'er," Abe said.

Zeph through up an XY grid on screen. He placed two points on the grid. "So the most direct way to get from point A to point B is to join them with a diagonal line, right?" He drew that line with his finger, and it appeared on screen as a bright blue line.

"Basic navigation," Ramirez. "The fastest route between two points is a line."

"Okay, but is it really faster?" Zeph asked.

Tai groaned. "How can direct not be faster?"

"Well I appreciate your question, Tai." Zeph was really enjoying himself now.

"I'm going to appreciate the concavity of your skull soon," Kelly said.

Zeph thought about that one for a bit. "But skulls protrude outward so that would be conve—ooooh." He raised his hands. "Okay, okay. So when is faster not faster? When one of the axes is time." He labeled the X axis as 'time.' He then drew a line straight down from point A. It glowed bright green.

"I'm traveling closer to point B, even though it is not a direct path to B, agree?"

"Yes, but you're going the longer way around," Ramirez said.

"But X is time and I haven't moved any time." The room was quiet.

"Perpendicular," Ramirez finally said. "It's because you are moving perpendicular."

"Exactly!" Zeph clapped. "If you could magically move in a way that time was perpendicular to your traversal, you could move around without ever taking any time to do so. And that is the fastest way to get from point A to point B." He swiped the grid away and then returned to the astral map.

"Now let's get real complicated. Imagine if we could travel all four dimensions within Ring space and set them all to be perpendicular without fear of being reduced to our constituent molecules." While Ring space was strange, it still adhered to mundane rules such as the conservation of mass, Dax knew. "We could move in directions across the dimensional topography that . . ."

"Eigenvalues zero dot zero dot zero dot zero," Dax said.

"Exactly." Zeph pulled the nav modules display and overlaid it on the astral map, his console starting to crunch the calculations. Then he rotated the display once more. All the portals aligned into a concentric spiral funnel that converged into one point. "Not the end. The beginning. Or rather the Origin."

"So that's where the rally beacon is directing us to?" Ramirez was already pulling up rally protocols on her wristcom.

Abe answered this one. "It asks all Cooperative forces capable of wedge travel, to converge at this staging area." He pointed to a destination inside Ring space. "It's the top, err, pinnacle of the funnel."

"But this was days ago," Dax said. "Will they even be there still?"

"Emergency rally protocol dictates that a trailing beacon will be left behind that will contain the next jump coordinates," Ramirez read, "that will decrypt to a valid OC armed forces ID."

They sat in silence.

"Zeph. you sure that this will work?" Dax asked, stern. "Because if it doesn't—"

"It will work." All the levity and obtuseness left him. The astrogator console beeped, indicating that the data had been successfully uploaded. "It has to."

Silence again.

A second beep broke the silence and the astral map inverted, forming a two-sided logarithmic funnel. Zeph placed a finger on one side, "Us, real space." Then the other, and a thin green line, which ran directly through the funnel, appeared. "It, Ring space"

Dax looked everyone in the eye and received a nod in return. "Well, that was a very good presentation, at least."

Zeph smiled. "Presentation matters." He started spinning up the coordinates in the nav computer.

"One question—how'd you get the processing power to map that out? Surely the nav console isn't powerful enough to make those calculations in real time. I mean, it takes about half an hour for it to model the astral map of a local system."

"Oh, well since the Tactum seems to operate while the Ring is open, I slaved Tai's and your command console to mine. Triple the processing power."

Dax contemplated on the perverse irony that he was, at this point, still not used to not having the Tactum and at the same time had already forgotten to be comfortable with it.

Within a few moments the crew was strapped in. The main display was consumed by the event horizon of the Ring.

"You know," Kelly said, her voice tinny over the wristcom. "There's only one issue about your theory there, Zeph."

Zeph's head popped up over the nav console. "What, no. Impossible."

"You said, 'there's only one thing in this universe that doesn't operate under relativistic laws.'"

"Go on."

"But that isn't true. Until recently there were two things that applied to."

"The Ring and…?"

Kelly took a breath. "The Tactum."

"Aww hell," Dax said. "I'm already having the darndest time trying to think through this map in four dimensions. I don't need you to add ANOTHER dimension of complexity to it." He gritted his teeth and pointed to Zeph to across his console.

"Punch it!"

CHAPTER 30

It was a decidedly odd sensation, Dax concluded, to experience an event horizon within the Ring space. Everything was opposite of the way it should be. What would opening an event horizon inside an event horizon even look like? Matter would be simultaneous drawn in and pushed out. Like a . . .

"Like an inverted funnel . . ."

"What did you say Cap?" Tai asked, looking away from her tactical display.

"Oh nothing. Astrophysics. Nothing you would understand."

Tai gave him a dour look. "Sure Cap."

"Ooh, that reminds me," Dax said, flipping on the onboard comms. "This is your Captain speaking. We soon will be leaving . . ." he paused. "Uh, we'll be leaving nowhere, and, for members of our Frequent Apocalypse Miles program, you will be earning 0 relativistic lightyears on today's jump to…also nowhere?" He turned to Zeph. "I mean that's the plan, right Zeph? Sometime this century?"

Zeph, upping Tai, gave him a death glare, which was exquisitely lit by the console's orange glow. "Look Captain, just because you yell 'punch it' doesn't mean the nav computer can just magically calculate the precise Eigenvalues too-o-o-ohhhwow."

Tai and Dax looked at each other, and then at Zeph in turn. "Oh wow, what?"

"Approach vector confirmed to within zero point zero zero zero zero zero one accepted deviation." Zeph gulped. "And I'm pretty sure that is just a rounding error. Make for one hundred by one hundred. Exactly."

"Let's do this then. Tetra voids." Dax attempted to go hands-on.

"Hold. Hold. No correction needed. Approach vector confirmed."

"Zeph, I wasn't making those corrections."

"Approach vector confirmed. Eigen deviations have harmonized to nth order—wait what?"

"I said, I wasn't hands-on!"

Tai interjected. "Then who in the voids is flying this ship?"

"It's them." Zeph glanced at his console, almost

mesmerized. "The Kyrie is now entering the Ring space's quantum uncertainty field well."

Dax braced himself, taking a deep breath, as he felt the ship slip in the well. Like being on the peak of a roller coaster as it came to a brief, rickety halt. And for one moment, you could look over the precipice, and, with horror, contemplate the fall for the duration of one breath.

Dax exhaled.

And then inhaled again.

Tai was the first to speak up. "You know, for instantaneous deconstruction and reconstruction across a quantum tunnel, this is taking a very long time."

"It's odd." Zeph said, trying to make heads or tails of his display. "I mean we're moving, but we're not." He ran a few calculations. "Odd. Constant speed. No acceleration. We are traveling at exactly the speed of light here."

"You'd think," Dax said, "that breaking the laws of physics would feel more…fast."

"One, fast isn't an appropriate adjective in that usage." Zeph said, raising a finger, and then removing his inertia straps. "And second, Einstein states that within frames of relative velocity, there is no possible way to differentiate between that frame of reference and moving still."

Dax thought hard on this. "Fast…ly?"

"I think the word you are looking for Captain is 'disconcerting.'"

"Or possibly 'jarring,'" Ramirez said. "Is Zeph correct, are we at constant velocity?"

"Apparently," Dax said, tugging at his own inertia straps cautiously. "You falling for it?"

Ramirez responded by unstrapping herself and standing up. "I'll trust the one that can use an adjective correctly. And knows astrophysics."

Tai was already floating from her chair and was checking the ship structural readouts. "Kyrie reads constant vee as well, Cap. Even odder, the external sensors don't even detect any spatial disturbances or friction."

Dax's head officially exploded. They were traveling through a higher order dimension, at the speed of light, without experiencing any of the dangers that would be a threat at even small fractions of the speed of light, like Wedge Drive. No random dust particles to mess with Newton's law of motion, no friction.

"It's like the Kyrie is an ice skater and the universe is a perfectly smooth lake over 4th dimension space. And where just cutting," Zeph said, making a slicing motion with his hands through the air, "through the universe we know. Barely skimming it. Barely slowed down by it."

Dax shivered, and not from the ice imagery. Everything he had been thought as a pilot said this was wrong. All of this should be wrong.

"Frame of reference. Frame of reference." He said to

himself, over and over.

"Oh no," he heard Kelly say, as if from a distance, "did alien technology contradicting the laws of known physics break the captain as well?"

"He'll get over it," Tai said. "I think we're good to drop these blast shields if we reading constant v."

"I look forward to the view," Bik said. "I rarely have had the privilege to see real space folded. Our Cooperative Marine berths on a ship are traditionally in the belly. No windows."

The entire conversation took place around Dax. He was floating, above his physical form, not tethered to anything.

Ramirez approached him and took his hands. "You five by five there, Cap?"

"Eh, I'm not sure to be honest." He shook himself. Or rather, his physical form tried to shake itself. "I learned a lot of things in flight school. How to use my instruments as my eyes when there was no visibility. How to cut my losses when approaching bingo fuel. But most of all, I learned to trust my instincts. I didn't learn how to deal with the end of the known universe. I can't fly my way through this by the seat of my pants."

"Ooooh, are we dropping the blast shields?" He heard Kelly say.

"Hey, hey, your instincts have gotten us this far. Don't forget that," Ramirez said. He could feel himself grounding. "Your pants are just fine." She patted his butt with grave seriousness. He felt his feet touch the ground.

"Thanks." He released a sigh. And then grasped Ramirez's hand. "Thanks."

Tai released the blast shield to the deck.

Something was wrong.

"Isn't it supposed to be blue?"

Bloodred light streamed in through the observation ports.

"Doppler shift?" Zeph suggested.

Dax propelled himself to his command console.

"I'm not familiar with that term."

"It's also called 'redshift.'"

"I mean, okay it's red, but—"

He looked at his console read outs. Everything was normal.

"Well it's a phenomenon where wavelengths of energy increase, i.e. approach the red side of spectrum when objects are moving apart or—"

"—Or moving closer. In a fastly manner." Dax finished. Everyone stared at him. "Zeph, on my command, disconnect the nav computer from ALL Tactum feeds. Everyone, drop suits and battle stations. I'm going hands-on."

CHAPTER 31

On Dax's mark, Zeph disconnected the nav computers from the Tactum and the ship immediately came to a halt. Well, immediately wasn't a good enough word. At one moment, the Kyrie was travelling at the constant velocity of the speed of light. And then the next moment, it was traveling at the constant velocity of zero. Which was a physical improbability. Bodies had to experience acceleration to change velocities.

"Was that as weird as I thought it was?" Dax asked.

"I smell a trap," Abe said.

"Inertial read outs confirm, we went from C to 0 with no measurable values in between." Tai looked at Dax from her console. She knew that something was off as well.

Dax was getting really tired of physical impossibilities becoming the norm around his ship. It made Kyrie anxious.

"Let's get visuals on the display." A wash of red appeared on screen. "Zeph, can we clean this up?"

"With what? We just disconnected from the T feed. I have no data to clean."

Dax pounded his fist on his console and then pointed straight at Zeph. "Did we not, just a matter of cycles ago, survive a collapsing solar system WITHOUT the Tactum?"

Zeph stared at him blankly for a moment and then grimaced. "Whoopsiedoodoo boss. I'm going to ping on active ladar."

They waited a few precious seconds as the Kyrie used the alternating electromagnetic pings from its ladar to make an interpolation of their surroundings.

An image resolved on screen.

"What are we looking at?" Ramirez's voice came over the comm, strapped in on one of Kyrie's gun consoles.

"It looks like . . ." Tai said, squinting at the image. "Debris?"

"It's not a fine enough resolution to tell." Dax said. He scratched at the stubble that had grown to an irritating length on his face. He had not yet found a convenient time or place to shave during the end of the world. "Let's use a beacon transmitter?"

"Loading." Tai went through the sequence that would arm the beacon in the Kyrie's launch pod, equipped with ladar equipment. "Beacon away."

Ladar, and its old timey compatriot radar, worked on signal differentiation, using the time difference between signal generation and bounce back to interpolate a distance. However, if the calculation could be made between two points, the interpolation resolution was improved. The drone reached optimal distance—far enough away from the Kyrie so that image resolution could be superb but not far enough to prevent two-way communication between the ship and the drone.

The images came in.

"More debris. Exciting, Captain," Tai said as the images were interpolated and processed. "But in higher definition."

"Wait. Stop there." Ramirez said. "Can you enhance that?"

"Uh sure," Zeph said. "By shooting a higher energy ladar at it."

"You can't just enhance the image?"

"This isn't a crime procedural holo. I can only display as much data as I have. And with us cut off from that Tactum—" He shot Dax an accusatory look "—this is it Sarge."

"Just do it." Dax said. "I have a feeling."

"A brown pants feeling?" Tai asked.

But they waited in patient silence for the ladar to shoot a higher resolution beam at Ramirez's location.

It resolved into a durasteel structure with a strange logo

on it.

"What is it?" Dax said.

"Rotate it." Ramirez said. "I mean, you CAN do that, right Zeph?"

"I mean, we'll lose some fine image resolution, but it's not like changing the orientation of an image requires me to create data that doesn't exist." He pinched the image on his nav console with two fingers and rotated, and the image on the display did likewise. "So yes, I CAN do that."

Tai gasped. "No, that's the—"

"OCISHC." Our Cooperative Inner Systems: High Command. The body that included the Admiral of the OCN and the OCMC, and the Supreme Marshall of the OCAF, Our Cooperative Armed Forces. And the Emperor. "And even worse, that's a Raider."

OCISHC's clunky acronym was often expressed as "high seas" And the fleet assigned to High Command of the Inner Systems was known as the Raiders, as in Raiders of the high seas.

"That's what I saw, but the fleet identifier confirms it. That's a battle cruiser from the Raider fleet."

The Raider fleet was possibly the most well-armed fleet in the universe known to mankind. And as more ladar came in, the picture became clearer: they were in a ship graveyard.

Not all from High Command. Sixth Colonial, Fifth Inner, Twenty Fourth Mercantile, Sixteenth Marine Expeditionary.

Tai and Ramirez recognized markers from eight other fleets within the Cooperative.

"What happened here?" Zeph asked.

"Obviously the staging rally did not go well," Dax said.

"Wait, Zeph, pause, right there." Tai said, pointing to the screen.

Ramirez looked closer. "No way, is that really?—"

"PRF."

"People's Republic Fleet?" Dax asked. "Is that what happened here? A showdown between the Cooperative and the Republic?"

"It doesn't lead from destruction pattern here. See those two destroyers over there?" Tai shifted the map view. "They crashed into each other, so the superstructures are entangled, but they are both oriented in the same direction." She changed the feed type to mass spectrometer. "Also, it appears as if the same attack pierced both of them. This suggests more of a combat in formation instead of against each other."

"I agree," Ramirez said. "The evidence suggests that this was a joint operation between the Cooperative and the Republic."

"But joint against what?" Dax searched his memory. "I mean, the Cooperative and the Republic haven't joined forces since . . ."

"Since never." Ramirez. "Not since the colonial divide."

"So what in the universe could make the two biggest

governments in existence lay aside their differences and fight together?"

The entire cabin was silent.

And then the universe pulsed.

Their beacon transmitter was instantly destroyed. Their sensors were overloaded and soon were displaying loss of signal.

Then a voice came over their speakers. "And what do we have here?"

CHAPTER 32

Every alarm on Kyrie was immediately set off.

"What are we getting hit with, Tai?"

"Pretty much everything?" With a swipe, Tai brought the alarm HUD on the main view screen. "If we've got an alarm for it, we're getting a warning for it. Radiological, electrical, magnetic…you name it, it's blaring."

"Obviously not all those warnings are authentic," Ramirez said.

"Obviously. But something is wrong here." Dax said. "Not to mention THE RANDOM VOICE THAT JUST CAME OVER COMMS!"

"Abe, Zeph, I need you to clear up our comm frequencies, RFN. We're basically blind out here."

"We're trying, boss," Zeph said, "but the signal parity is so dense, the algorithms either filter everything out or leave all the noise in."

100% loss or 100% noise. As if someone was trying to blind them. Dax felt an itch between his shoulder blades.

"And what do we have here? What is your name, little one?"

"Tai, where is that voice coming from?"

"Cap, you tired of hearing 'everywhere'?"

"I just wish I was asking, 'Oh Tai, where are all the pretty ladies that want to buy me drinks.' 'Oh Captain, are you tired of me saying—'"

"Boss, I got something weird here." Zeph interrupted Dax's hypothetical.

"Give it to me, Zeph."

Blink

Every alarm on Kyrie was immediately set off.

"What are we getting hit with, Tai?"

"Pretty much everything? If we got an alarm for it, we're getting a warning for it."

"Obviously not all those warnings are authentic," Ramirez.

"Obviously. But something is wrong here. Not to mention the random . . ."

"Speak little one. Tell me what you have seen out there."

". . . random voice." Dax shook his head. Déjà vu? "Abe,

Zeph, why haven't we cleaned up our comm frequencies?

"We're trying boss," Zeph said.

"Try harder! We're basically blind out here."

"The signal parity is so dense, the algorithms either filter everything out or leave all the noise in."

100% loss or 100% noise. As if someone was trying to blind them. Dax felt an itch between his shoulder blades.

"Tai where is that voice coming from?"

"Everywhere."

"I'm getting really tired of hearing—"

"Captain, I got something weird here." Zeph interrupted Dax's tirade.

Dax turned in his command chair to look at his Astrogator.

"So I tried backtracking the voice and—"

"And?"

"Well that led nowhere."

Dax grunted. "Okay."

"So I tried interpolating the signal source."

"And? Nothing again?"

"No, I got everywhere."

"This better be leading to SOMEWHERE, Zeph."

"So I tried interpolating the destination."

"Wait, you can do that?"

"No, you shouldn't be able to. Normal electromagnetic signals propagate as a wave. But this signal, or this tight beam, is actually curving and redirecting to a specific location."

"Where?"

Zeph pointed to the astrogation module. No, wait, he was pointing to something in it. He was pointing to—

Blink

Every alarm on Kyrie was immediately set off.

"What are we getting hit with, Tai"

"Everything."

"I'm getting really tired of hearing that—"

"Obviously not everything. Not all those warnings can be authentic."

"Obviously. But something is wrong here?" He said. No, he asked.

"Truly your eyes have been opened little one."

"Not to mention the random voice. Abe, Zeph, why haven't we cleared up our comm frequencies?"

"We're trying boss," Zeph said.

"Try harder! We're basically blind out here."

"The signal parity is so dense, the algorithms either filter everything out or leave all the noise in."

100% loss or 100% noise. As if someone was trying to blind them. Dax felt an itch between his shoulder blades.

"Tai?" He began.

"Where is that voice coming from?" Tai asked.

"Yes…wait, no, I mean give me tactical display."

Tai threw the display on the view screen.

"Give me friend or foe overlay."

The entire screen glowed blue with friendly signatures.

"Obviously not all those friend signals are authentic." Ramirez said.

"Yes, but you already used that phrase this repetition."

"I did? When?"

"In the beginning of . . ." Dax shook his head. What had he been saying?

"Captain, I got something weird here." Zeph interrupted Dax's thoughts.

Dax turned in his command chair to look at his Astrogator.

"You tried backtracking the voice?" he asked. No, he said.

"Uh, yes?"

"And that led nowhere."

Zeph grimaced "Uh yes. But how did you—"

"So you tried interpolating the signal source."

Zeph nodded.

"And you got everywhere as the source. And then I said 'this better be leading to SOMEWHERE, Zeph.'"

"You did?"

"So you tried interpolation the destination."

"Wait, I can do that?" Zeph started punching commands into his console.

"Yes you can, because—"

"Oh wowowyeah, the tight beam is actually curving and redirecting to a specific location."

"Specifically where Zeph?"

He pointed to the astrogation module.

"Use your words." He stared hard at Zeph.

Zeph mouthed a word.

Blink

Every alarm on Kyrie was immediately set off.

Tai brought up a display. "Wow, that's everything. It looks like if we have a sensor for it, the alarm is currently . . ." The conversation flowed around Dax like water.

"Obviously not everything. Not all of those can be authentic."

Ramirez had already used that phrase this repetition. Or had she?

"Boss," Zeph said. "We're trying to clean up the comm frequencies but the signal parity is so dense, the algorithms either filter out everything or leave all the noise in."

100% loss or 100% noise. As if someone was trying to blind them. Dax felt an itch between his shoulder blades.

"Yes, you see now with such clarity. Show me more."

"Not to mention the random voice."

Everyone looked at him. Oh, he had said his line out of

sequence.

"Which, by the way, Zeph, you can trace the destination of."

"Wait what?" Zeph said, starting to punch commands into his console. "That shouldn't be possible. Electromagnetic signals propagate as a wave . . ."

He ignored the rest of what Zeph was saying. He'd figure it out.

"Tai…give me tactical display."

Tai threw the display on the view screen.

"Do you remember that story of Epsilon rebels, during the Reconstructions, and how they were getting shipments through the Cooperative Blockade?"

Ramirez and Tai nodded. They both would have been active duty during that time.

"They duped the Friend and Foe sensors, and then overloaded the sensor arrays," Ramirez said. "And they would send the packages using inertia-only sub-orbital drops. It meant everything coming in had to be dry sealed."

Ramirez made a blanching face. "Imagine living only on reconstituted food for three years."

"But it was clever, wasn't it? A very low-tech solution to a high-tech problem. Tai, give me a friend and foe overlay."

The tactical display screen lit up in blue friendly signatures.

"What does it mean?" Tai asked.

100% friends or 100% foes. Dax felt an itch between his shoulder blades.

"Dax, I found it, I found it! Ohwowowow. It's the data structure. From the comms array in Gamma."

"What does it mean?" Tai asked. Again. Twice this repetition.

"Only one way to find out." Dax turned to Zeph and Abe. "Zeph, disconnect the Nav computer from the Tactum feed. Abe, set the sensors to filter all readings from the T spectrum."

On Dax's mark, Zeph disconnected the Nav computers from the Tactum and the ship immediately came to a halt. Well, immediately wasn't a good enough word. At one moment, the Kyrie was traveling at the constant velocity of the speed of light. And then the next moment, it was traveling at the constant velocity of zero. Which was a physical improbability. Bodies had to experience acceleration to change velocities.

"Was that as weird as I thought it was?" Dax asked.

"It is amazing how easy it is to play with the minds of those so simple."

"Not to mention," Dax said, "the random voice that just came over comms!"

"I smell a trap," Abe said.

"Inertial read outs confirm, we went from C to 0 with no measurable values in between." Tai looked at Dax from her console. She knew that something was off as well.

Dax was getting really tired of physical impossibilities becoming the norm around his ship. It made Kyrie anxious.

"Let's get visuals on the display." A wash of Red appeared on screen. "Zeph, can we clean this up?"

"With what? We just disconnected from the T feed. Anyway, the signal parity is so dense, the algorithms either filter everything out or leave all the noise in."

100% loss or 100% noise. As if someone was trying to blind them. Dax felt an itch between his shoulder blades.

"Tai, give me tactical display. Give me a friend or foe overlay."

Tai threw the display on screen. It glowed blue. Wasn't it glowing red just a moment ago?

"Obviously not all those friends signals are authentic."

"Yes, but you already used that phrase this repetition." Didn't she? "Or was that in the beginning of the last . . ."

"What did you say, Cap?" Tai asked.

Dax shook his head. "You remember that story about Epsilon rebel, during the Reconstructions, and how . . ."

"The Epsilon rebels were getting shipments through the blockade," Tai finished. "Yes, because you told us that story already during this repetition."

"I did?"

Blink

Every alarm on the Kyrie immediately set off.

"Zeph, disconnect the Nav computer from the Tactum feed! Set the sensor to filter all readings from the T spectrum!"

Zeph disconnected the Nav computer and the ship immediately came to halt. No, wait, it spun up. It was a decidedly odd sensation, Dax concluded, to experience an event horizon within the Ring space. Everything was opposite of the way it should be.

Blink

Every alarm on the Kyrie immediately set off.

"I take back the part where I called this a plan," Ramirez said.

"What's not to like," he said. "I understand it might not fit the marine SOP but—"

"If there was a name for a thing that was the opposite of a plan, it would be this thing."

"Now you are just trying to hurt my feelings, Ramirez."

Blink

Every alarm on the Kyrie immediately set off.

"Cap, you five by five there?" Tai asked.

"I can't shake it, Tai."

"Hey, leave it to us. You ain't the only one fighting for our lives here, okay?"

Blink

Every alarm on the Kyrie immediately set off.

"Are you hands-on?" Tai asked.

"You bet your chips I am," he said.

"I hate it when you say 'bet'; it brings back a lot of bad memories."

"We're deviating a bit from the approach vector, Cap," Zeph reminded him. "You do know that if we approach the Ring even a single azimuth off, the Eigen forces involved will—"

"You," Dax glared at Zeph, "are going to lecture me about an uncertain death when a highly probable one is in front of us in the shape of TWO giant orbital standoff stations and the metric tons of ammunition and ordnance they have between them?"

Zeph paused. "Boss," he started, almost timidly, "you do know that just because the forces exist in a 'quantum uncertainty field,' doesn't mean we are uncertain about them."

"Yes, yes Observer, something something. I passed navigation physics." He hadn't.

Blink

There was no sound. He was on Pica and for a moment the galaxy was completely silent and still. He was in a bedroom. A modestly furnished one. There was a black-haired girl in bed next to him. He had danced with her in one of those dockside nightclubs. She had blue eyes.

How did he know? He turned her over, to confirm.

Her face was a complete blank. It was okay. She was probably dead now. But couldn't he at least remember her name, voids?

"What was your name, little one?" the girl with the blank face asked. In her hand she held a bird. The bird had a small tag chained to its leg. The tag read "Kyrie."

"Who are you?" Dax asked.

The girl turned to face him, and then cocked her head inquisitively, which was decidedly eerie, without facial features.

"Ah," the girl said, the voice emanating from one source now, "so, you have arrived."

"Arrived where?" Dax asked. He looked around.

"Oh, don't try to make sense of your surroundings." She put Kyrie's cage down on a dresser. Had there always been a cage? "It is simply a construct that your mind can comprehend." No, he had been sure that it had been in her hand previously.

"So where am I?" He reached out to touch the bird cage,

but the girl grabbed his hand before he could reach it.

"You are at the Pinnacle. Of Arbitration."

"And you are?"

"Arbitration, Pinnacle of."

That made Dax frown. "I'm not sure I heard you ri—"

"Oh, you heard me right," Arbitration said. "It's just your meat sounds can only convey a limited level of nuance."

"Meat sounds?" Dax felt at his jaw and lips, suddenly self-conscious.

"You push air through a meat tube and then form it by slapping meat together." She made a talking gesture with her hand. "It's quaint."

"Hey . . ." Dax thought about it for a moment. He wasn't sure if he was supposed to be insulted or not.

"So tell me meatling, what did you all accomplish with half a millennia with our gift?"

"What gift?" He sat down on the bed, keeping the bird cage and Arbitration in his line of sight."

"What gift, it says," Arbitration said. She tilted her head back and chortled. "Why, the gift of instantaneous communication AND travel, of course?"

Dax thought for a moment. "You mean the Rings and the Tactum . . ."

". . . came from my masters. What does your species say? 'She giveth and she taketh away.'" She made a turning gesture with her hand and the walls and roof of the little room fell away, revealing a vast void. Dax stood up from the bed. "When you had Her gifts, did you use them with care? Did you unite your species, work towards the good of all, towards mutual prosperity?" Arbitration approached him, circling him, like a predator. "Or did you divide, scheme, work towards the undermining of your fellow insects?"

"I…we . . ." Dax looked within himself. He had attempted to save those he could, where he could. But he was equally guilty of destruction. As an individual he was decent. As a species, what were they? Where they a net positive or negative in the galaxy?"

"I have decided," Arbitration said. "I have reached an arbitration."

Dax just looked at her, inching around her proximity. "How?"

"Very impartially, I promise you. I simply captured a sample consciousness into a reverse temporal stream and experienced your timeline recursively."

"Whose consciousness?"

"All of those who dared enter the pinnacle of course."

Dax gulped. "What happened to them?"

"The small sample size of your crew has not significantly altered the median. The end result will be the same: I will advise my masters that She should sanitize you from the Galaxy." She sighed. "One day, we will find a species worthy of our gifts." She paused, and captured Dax in an eyes stare.

"Unfortunately, today is not that day."

Dax lunged. Arbitration took a step back in surprise, but it wasn't her that Dax aimed at. He got hold of the bars on the birdcage and rip—

Blink.

Every. Damn. Alarm. On the Kyrie was immediately. Set. Off.

"Tai, I'm going hands-on!"

"If we got an alarm for it, we're getting a." She stopped. Shook her head. "What?"

"I said I am going hands-on! In the meantime, throw up tactical, IFF overlay." The screen glowed blue. Ramirez opened her mouth as if to speak. "And no, Ramirez, obviously not all those alarms NOR all those friend signatures are authentic." He turned to her, looking her straight in the eye. "Just because you haven't had a chance to say that yet, this repetition."

She gave him quizzical look, and then nodded. "I take back the part where I called this a plan."

"Zeph, do we still have the offline maps for the Gamma ring?"

"Negative Cap. The signal parity is so dense, the algowhaaat?"

"Yeah, ignore that, that algorithms either filter everything out or leave all the noise in anyway. Do you have the offline maps for the approach vectors for the Gamma ring?"

"You mean the auto calculated ones?"

"No, don't use any auto eigenvalues or approach vectors. I want you to create a new approach, from scratch, without using ANY computer that is connected to a T frequency."

"Well to do that—"

"Yes I know. Abe!" He turned to the marine.

"Yes Far—I mean Captain," Abe said.

"Abe set the sensors to filter all readings from the T spectrum."

Zeph started keying in new approach vectors. "Okay, make for 72 by 128."

Dax maneuvered the Kyrie.

"Approach vector confirmed to within zero point zero point. Wait." Dax saw Zeph blink his eyes against the orange glare. "No, confirmed within eight point zero point zero. Make for sixty-three by ninety-seven. Coming about now. Correction, Correction." He blinked again and also shook his head, as if he was trying to get rid of some after image in his eye.

"Abe, come over here. Can you confirm this reading for me? I swear I keep seeing two different numbers."

"Uh,"

"Just tell me the number, and I'll do the vector corrections in my head."

"24 by 156."

"Voids, we overcorrected. We're outside more than ten deviations. We were going to get voiding butchered by the event horizon." He closed his eyes, and his fingers seemed to be typing on some keyboard that was invisible to Dax. Or, maybe it was more like playing a sonata on an invisible piano.

"Captain, come about again, make for one fifty by fifty-four."

Dax made the necessary corrections.

"Approach vector confirmed. Within four point one accepted deviation."

"Is that within the none uncertain death kind yet, Astrogator?"

Zeph smiled. "Not even voiding close."

"This is your captain speaking," Dax said over the comms. "We will soon be leaving this pocket temporal aberration that we seem to have been caught in and will be heading for normal space." He stopped. "Well, more normal than the space we are in now, at least. We are within . . ." he turned to Zeph.

Zeph did the calculations quickly. "Um zero point one five ohohOH, that's good enough!"

"Good enough, our Astrogator says."

"I'm pretty certain." Zeph said.

"Thanks for flying post-Apocalyptic Air," Dax said, continuing, "where we make precise space-time intersectionalities with quantum uncertainty fields, with pretty certain approach vectors. It might be the end of the world, but not the end of our sense of humor."

He turned to Zeph and Abe, who both nodded.

"Punch it!"

Zeph keyed in the disconnect commands, while Abe recalibrated the broad-spectrum filters, just as Dax pierced the event horizon of the Ring. Well, hopefully the Ring. Even though he was pretty sure that they had already gone through the Ring once? But surely not during this repetition, right?

The display screen went dark, leaving after images of IFF red and blue designators.

They entered the stream.

The screen came back to life, replacing the after images with a sea of red foe designators.

Alarms on the Kyrie immediately set off.

"Radiological warnings! Missiles inbound!" Tai said, reading from her tactical screen. "All the surrounding structures are sounding off as foe!"

"Ramirez, get those guns manned. Tai, can you trace the sources of the radiologicals?"

"They're coming from voiding everywhere!"

"I'm getting really tired of . . ."

"I know, I know."

"Hammers!" Dax felt the sting from his knuckles punching the command console. "Evasive maneuvers, Kelly I need you to—"

"Why have the insects burned out your eyes and cut out your tongue, little one?"

CHAPTER 33

Dax brought the Kyrie engines to full power, moving blindly before Zeph could crunch an appropriate scram vector.

"Zeph, I need interpolation as soon as possible onscreen. Tai, I need evasive packages."

"Working on it!" Both said, getting their nav consoles to start chugging through the immense data that usually the Tactum's bandwidth and networking resources would assist with.

Zeph got there first, giving Dax a very sketchy interpolation of the debris around them. Emphasis on sketchy. There large polygonal spaces of just empty data. They had been so focused on identifying the destroyed ships around them that they had forgotten to take a clear scan of the surrounding space before Arbitration had burnt out their comm sensor.

"This is not looking good, Cap" Tai said. "I have radiologicals from seven different ships. It looks that Arbiter bastard is controlling several of them at a time, possibly all of them out here."

"And we're low on fuel and countermeasures," Bik said.

"Ramirez," Dax said, gritting his teeth as he had to dodge around the hull of a battle cruiser that wasn't on Zeph's interpolation. "Any ship out there look familiar to you?" he asked.

She thought for a while. "The Reagan," she said. "The Marine Expeditionary missile destroyer. I served on her a few PCSs ago."

"Do you think we can handshake with their FnF and targeting systems?"

"I know the general OCMC frequencies, sure."

"Good, I got an idea. Might even be a plan."

Dax lost one of the ballistic missiles by flying through the empty hull of a Republican super carrier. The bay was meant to house a Fortress Bomber but it was still a tight fit for the Kyrie, hands-on and blind as they were.

"We aren't going to need a missile to kill us if your flying does it before they reach us." Bik said from his gunnery position.

"You stick to shooting big guns and I'll stick to flying ships, big guy." Dax said. "You got that trajectory for me,

Zeph?"

"It's rough, but I can feed it to your—"

"Never mind about that, just put it on screen." Dax squinted at the 3-D overlay that showed an arcing path to the Reagan. He overshot the ideal trajectory and put her in a lateral spin. When the nose was pointed approximately perpendicular to the apex of the arc, he hit the retro thrusters and headed straight for the Ronald Reagan. Before they collided, however, Dax pulled the Kyrie into steep climb and ejected a beacon transmitter.

"Starting handshake!" Ramirez said at the same time Tai called out, "Missiles incoming!"

"Are you all just going to stand around and not shoot your guns?" He turned to the rest of the crew. They started firing immediately.

The Kyrie was a lightning bug, flying erratically through the empty space and all her guns firing a defilade of flak around it.

"I'm splash one!" Kelly said, as her turret took out a missile.

"Me as well!" Bik said

"That still leaves," Dax pretended to count on his fingers, "A lot!"

"Captain, I'm losing handshake signal."

"Roger." He flipped the Kyrie on its back and headed straight for the Ronald Reagan again.

"I think one more pass should do," Ramirez said.

"Good, because I think that's all she's got in her," Dax said.

"I'm splash four," Tai said.

"Splash two here," Kelly said.

"Countermeasures got two as well," Abe read from his readout. "But we don't got much of those left."

"I'm still splash one," Bik said, with a grimace.

"Where are you?" Dax said, mostly to himself. As he brought the Kyrie in for another pass.

"One more," Dax said. "Where are you, where are you…"

The missile came out of the ladar shadow, almost haughtily announcing itself on the tactical display: here I am, witness me.

"Ramirez, betting the pot on you," he said, and pulled the Kyrie into a severe dive.

"I told you," Ramirez said, gritting her teeth against the G-forces, "you make me nervous every time you make a gambling reference."

"Dax . . ." Zeph said, his tone concerned, "you see that HUD warning right?"

"Starboard thruster in the red, yup, I'm banking on it,"

"What did I say about gambling refer—"

"Not a gambling reference! Now Ramirez!" The Kyrie's starboard retro thruster stalled and he banked her into an uncontrolled spin lateral to the deck of the Reagan. The missile was locked on. Established tone.

And was obliterated by a flak gun

"I got the Reagan's point defense slaved to our FnF system." Ramirez said, throwing her hands up in the air in an uncharacteristic moment of exultation.

"Good, because we're almost bingo fuel." Dax said. Soon the Kyrie would have no wings.

"I have 10 more radiologicals," Tai said. "No, wait, make that 20."

"We won't be able to hide here long," Ramirez said. "That blast has put the Reagan on a decaying orbit."

"No wait, make that, wow, voids, 40 in total."

"You know," Dax said, interrupting them all. "For something called 'Arbitration,' she doesn't seem very keen on arbitrating!"

"Pinnacle of Arbitration isn't really a 'she,' Cap," Zeph said.

"Do you want me use 'it'? Seems kind of rude." Dax said. "Not that I am opposed to being rude to this voiding thing."

"You stand in the presence, tiny voice."

Dax looked at the rest of the crew, making sure that they too had heard the voice. "Who are you calling tiny? The presence of what?"

Zeph leaned towards Dax and intoned in a whisper. "No, Dax, this thing is the place. It is the place."

"You stand in the presence. Arbitration will commence."

"No no no no . . ."

"Did Arbitration tell you," Zeph gulped.

Tai nodded. Ramirez and Dax looked at each other. "Voids," Dax said. They had apparently all had similar conversations with Arbitration.

"Sanitization has commenced."

"Dax," Tai said, turning her console to face. "I've got lock on. I'm reporting tone."

"How many missiles?"

"No, you don't understand. It's all the missiles, all the MAC turrets, all the railguns. Everything."

CHAPTER 34

Zeph turned to them all, voice solemn. "I think I can do this."

Dax looked Zeph in the eye, and Zeph looked back, not flinching. "Do it Zeph. I'm counting on you."

Zeph smiled. "Tai, can you hand over your slave session?" She swiped one of her console screen across to Zeph. "Can we get more handshakes here?"

"With what?" said Abe. "That was our last beacon."

Without looking, Zeph partitioned his screen, and swiped it to Abe. "Use the Reagan's. I need something big, lots of components."

"On it."

While Abe was searching the Freqs for any open handshakes and the rest of the crew manned the Kyrie's small guns, Zeph was quickly partitioning his screen down even further. Voids. Instead of feeding a firing solution into all of the Reagan's guns, he was giving each gun a programmed solution, making tiny adjustments as he refreshed the tactical maps and then switching to the next gun.

The hail of fire prevented most of the armaments heading their direction from doing real harm, with the crew-manned guns and some reserved flight maneuvers keeping them from what got through. But soon the hail became a drizzle. "Abe, I'm coming up empty on these guns, and the reserve bays are either destroyed or inaccessible, and I am not finding a successful handshake to any of the autoloaders."

"It's because they use t-drone autoloaders," Tai said.

"Voids." Zeph said. "Abe, what you got for me?"

"I have a…Fujimoto Class Super Carrier?"

"The Queen Raider herself?" Tai said.

"Tell me what the handshake gave you." Zeph said, still manning the remaining point defense guns.

"Point defense."

"No, not enough range."

"Mass Accelerator?"

"Too slow."

"Drone bay?"

"How many?"

"Hundreds."

"Perfect."

With grand keyboard strokes and swipes, Zeph flung the

Reagan's point defenses guns to Dax's console and took the Queen Raider's slaved drone bay.

He partitioned his console into two. Then again into four. Eight. Zeph kept partitioning more screens until Dax lost count, until they must have been untenable.

A torrent of drones exploded from the Queen's belly, all just pinpoints of light flying intricate patterns against the dark sky. And Zeph was flying each one, hands-on.

Zeph's fingers flew across the screen, playing a sonata of destruction. Some drones he directed to shoot down incoming long-range missiles, other drones baited and switched short range tracker missiles, deflecting high energy lasers, and others flew into their own death, using their tiny bodies as a weapon. But with every drone that was downed, Zeph brought more.

Dax missed a simple maneuver as one of the retro thrusters gave out from lack of fuel. The missile flew danger close to the Kyrie and hit the side of the Reagan, dislodging a large chunk of debris that exploded into a cloud of dangerous shrapnel heading for the Kyrie.

A swarm of drones split off from the main body and shielded them from most of the blast.

And for a few moments, it seemed that Zeph was winning. Winning against an ancient entity left behind by a cosmically advanced civilization to judge those who would attempt to follow in their footsteps. For a few moments, Zeph held his ground against that.

But then, was Zeph slowing? No…he wasn't slowing. Dax checked the tactical display himself. Zeph wasn't slowing down, the Raider Queen was running out of drones. Yes, Zeph was holding his own, but civilization did not become advanced without learning how to cheat.

All of Zeph's partitioned screens exploded with bright light and violently strobing patterns. Zeph screamed, his hands covering his eyes, but he was taken over by seizures and shakes, the screens having repositioned themselves around Zeph's face, looking like a mask of bright orange consoles blasting bright lights.

Dax leapt out of his command chair and rushed to Zeph's side to manually rip out the power source. Zeph collapsed to the ground.

"Where did that come from?' Dax said, searching around him, looking for the culprit. "How did it get in here?"

"You have blinded my little one, so I have returned the favor."

"It's coming from one of the beacons!" Kelly said, pointing to the arbitrary location where she believed the Reagan to be. "It must have found a free comm port and then hijacked the signal."

"Block it."

"Too late," Abe said. "It's already burned-out."

"Captain, you are going to want to take a look at this."

Tai said. "I just got eleven handshake requests."

"How did we find so many at once?"

"No, we received them. Over the radio frequencies. In the clear."

"What are they?"

Tai pulled up a tac screen. "Eleven different gun boats, all direct handshakes to their point defense guns."

Dax spent a second contemplating. A second they had earned because the Arbiter had needed to focus on his little T-port hooligans. He looked at the haphazard hornet nest that represented all the material heading his way. He looked at the eleven gunships blinking on his map,

Tai looked at him, concern in her eyes. "What are you thinking?"

Dax didn't respond. Just looked through the blast shield into the bloodred void around them.

"I'm going to chase the flop."

"Again?" Ramirez said. "With the card and gambling references?" She was repositioning Zeph's head on her jacket that she had made into a makeshift pillow. "I mean, I guess at this point, you aren't gambling with much. Just our lives and your ship, which we are pretty sure to lose in a few seconds anyway." Ramirez scrunched her face up and thought for a moment. "I like this plan."

"You don't even know if I have a plan!"

"I'm okay with that." She gave him a thumbs-up. Dax

returned it.

"Abe, Tai, spin up all eleven point defenses! Show me their firing solutions."

"Dax, the tactical computer is going to need ages to crunch out a safe path around eleven interwoven solutions. We'll burn out the ALS, if it hasn't already."

"No crunching! Just give me a visual representation."

Dax went hands on. The gunships started firing, melting all the incoming fire.

And for 23 glorious seconds, Dax flew like he never had before his entire life. The Kyrie was a blind ballerina, spinning and dipping almost effortless around the point defense patterns of the 11 ships that surrounded them. It rained radiological hellfire on the Kyrie, but none could penetrate the 11-deep point-defense fire.

Dax danced among the stars, among the fire, but he let none of it touch him.

Then the Kyrie stopped responding to his commands, the fuel finally spent.

Then the gun ship defenses fell silent. Probably hijacked through their unprotected T-ports.

A new cloud of destruction slowly made its way to the Kyrie. It was accompanied by a laugh over their intercom.

Then every alarm on the Kyrie immediately set off. Behind them, away from the Pinnacle of Arbitration, another fury of missiles, drones, and MAC rounds tore into the space between them.

He watched the two waves destroy each other.

Bright flashes of lights illuminated their view ports as ships resolved in their vicinity, providing a near constant stream of fire that took apart ships and defended the Kyrie from incoming arsenal. More ships jump signatures joined them.

"It's glorious," Tai said, a tear forming in the corner of her eye. "Look at them. Look at how they maneuver into covering fields of fire, as other ships take their places around them. Those are Cooperative ships working with Republic ships."

Dax was wordless, too exhausted to offer a comment, but he didn't let that stop him from watching the choreography destruction play out in front of him.

And, in almost a whisper, but with clarity as if he heard it in a quiet room, he heard the voice once more. The voice of the place.

You call her Kyrie. In one of your dead insect tongues, that would mean 'God's love,' would it not? She will not love you.

Then the voice fled.

CHAPTER 35

A voice came over Kyrie's radio. Not spooky all frequency voice, just a normal human voice coming over a normal comm frequency.

"Hello this is Admiral Kim, who am I speaking to?"

Dax looked around at his crew before cautiously picking up the comm. "This is Captain Sheppard of the OCSS Kyrie." The Kyrie was dead in the water. There was nothing he could do anyway if this new voice had ill intentions

"And what, perchance, where are you doing at the Pinnacle of Arbitration?"

Dax looked at Abe, who just shrugged. "We were…uh, you know…kinda just stumbled into it. Got turned around somewhere. Probably should have hung a left instead of a right at Gamma. Honest mistake." Dax paused, then hit a keystroke sequence on his command console. "I have sent you my OC ship codes. I am carrying critically wounded. Please authenticate in kind?"

"Boy, that don't mean a darn spit of a thing. I am Admiral Kim of the Human Allied Forces. But let me see if I can find some way to authenticate in kind."

Dax got a better look at the ships around them.

It was unlike any fleet Dax had ever seen. A Yamamoto super carrier being worked on by a Republican tug. A Cooperative light cruiser docked to a Republican medical platform.

Tai jumped in. "That's THE 5th Ring of the High Council next to a Republican Dreadnought. And look, that's a mixed wing of OCN Falcons and Republic Bandits flying cap around that supercarrier."

Lights flashed across the Kyrie's bow.

"What are they doing," Dax said, dropping the blast shields to get a better look.

"It's Morse code?" Abe said. "Yes, I'm pretty sure." He pulled up a window on his console and started recording the light sequence.

"What does it say?"

"It's asking," Abe said, "In Omicron Hold'em, what do you call two queens in your hand, and a king and a queen on the river?"

Dax thought for a moment, then smiled. "Abe, I need you to respond with exactly what I tell you, okay? And don't leave anything out." Abe looked at Dax expectantly "It's my fair lady, you salty Republican bastard."

When they stepped out of the airlock to the docking bay, they were greeted by guards led them through the super carrier.

"I still don't get the question," Ramirez said. "Is that the name of a hand of poker? Or is it a maneuver?"

They walked that the carrier's hallways. Just like in the tiny shuttle that brought them over, there was a mix of Republic and Cooperative bustling about. Abe stopped at an intersection and inspected a large bundle of fiber optic cable that ran the length of the deck until their escorts politely gestured them forward.

"Neither," Dax said. "It's from a rather famous scene in a movie. There is a special agent from the United Kingdom Royal Colonies Service and he's playing cards with an undercover People's Republic spy, and just when the Agent is about to beat the spy—"

They were interrupted by a woman in a resplendent admiral uniform.

"He pulls out his gun and says, 'It's my fair lady, you salty Republican bastard!.'" The woman in the admiral's uniform finishes. With a smile and a chuckle. "Please, allow me to show you our observation deck." He followed her and her small complement of aides through some very sterile, very white passageways. The pristine decor was only slightly marred by being haphazardly crisscrossed by even more fiber optic cables.

"I am High Admiral Ba'ang Kim, previously Rear Admiral, lower sword of the People's Republican Guard Fleet. I guess, by the rule of succession, I would be Grand Admiral now, but that is neither here nor there, is it?"

"But you're—"

"Republic? Yes, but even I can appreciate a good spy flick. A lot has happened since before you had your one on one grudge match at and with the Pinnacle of Arbitration. Most impressive by the way. We were watching it in relativistic real time, which unfortunately was about a light hour away. But I promise you, we mobilized a small strike force as soon as we could once we realized what was happening."

"And who is 'we' in this case?"

"Well, that is a complex question to answer, isn't it? 'We' is such a flexible term." She seemed to work her mouth around it, tasting. "It can be as grand as a President and her nation, a Governess and her planet, or even a Princess and her Shogunate." She looked at Tai.

"An Admiral and her fleet," Tai said in response.

"It can be as wide as you want," Admiral Ba'ang said. "Or it can be as small as you want, too. A company, a squadron, a small gang. Or the crew of one ship."

Dax said nothing. None of them did. They stood there in front of blast shields firmly in place on the observation deck.

"We have your Astrogator set up comfortably in the med bay." She paused. "'We' can be a collective word, or an exclusionary word. It can bring people together or pull them apart." She raised her hand to the blast shields but then retracted them, turning to look back at them. "Even with less than .5 percent of the population, and yes that's percent, projected to survive this catastrophe, I imagine there are still people out there who want to divide us even further."

"For me, there is only one distinction of 'We' that matters anymore." She raised one gloved finger. "'We' the human race. It is enough that you and I are the same species for me to take in your hurt, to defend you from the foreign and the unknown."

She turned to Ramirez. "Sergeant, I have gotten permission from the highest surviving Our Cooperative Marine command to absorb you in my chain of command." Her voice got quieter. "With your permission, I would like to relieve you of your burden."

Ramirez looked at Kim. Her face was severe. No, it was just the face she made as she tried to hold back tears. She warred with herself before she got her emotions in check. She lifted her wristcom and projected all the tags she had collected. The air between them exploded in golds and blues.

Kim lifted her wrist to receive them. "I relieve you,

Sergeant Theresa Ramirez, OCMC."

"I stand relieved, Admiral."

The marines gave a smart salute. The Admiral returned it. Then she turned and pressed a button.

The blast shields of the observation deck retracted, Dax stepped up to take in the view. Below him was an armada that was as vast as it was diverse. A showcase of humanity's diverse efforts to traverse the emptiness of space. Mostly military, but there was a respectable smattering of industrial ships and even some civilian. "Welcome, crew of the Kyrie," she said, "to the Human Fleet 'Salvation.' First, and, if we don't change things around fast, last of her kind."

Never miss a Future House release!

Sign up for the Future House Publishing email list:

http://www.futurehousepublishing.com/send-free-book/

Connect with Future House Publishing

www.facebook.com/FutureHousePublishing

twitter.com/FutureHousePub

www.youtube.com/FutureHousePublishing

www.instagram.com/FutureHousePublishing

ABOUT THE AUTHOR

J. T. Solo loves 1970's sci-fi covers. There's something about the idea of space travel that keeps him up at night (especially Fermi's Paradox). Although he's never been to space, he feels completely qualified to be an astronaut due to his attendance at space camp in the seventh grade. If he doesn't become a household name for his writing, he'd happily accept being the first man on Mars instead. J. T. (currently) lives on the west coast with his furry cat named Tribble.